Note:

Sale of this book without an official cover may be unauthorized; if you have purchased this book without a cover or a duplicate cover, it may have been bootlegged. The author did not receive payment for the sale of this book.

This novel is a work of fiction. Any resemblance to real people, living or dead, actual events, establishments, organizations', and/or locales are intended to give the fiction a sense of reality and authenticity. Other names, characters, places, and incidents either are products of the author's imagination or used fictitiously.

Published by:

Shameeka Williams c/o Hustle Bunny Books

P.O Box 3731

Hampton, VA 23663

ISBN: 978-0-692-002650

Copyright: TXu 1-622-521

I0562099

Acknowledgments

First, I have to thank god for blessing me and giving me the will, the patience and the drive because without him none of this would be possible. I want to thank everyone who believed in me from day one, I want to thank my children for being so understanding when mommy tuned them out many of nights while working on this book. I want to thank my mother Cassandra Williams for giving me the tools I needed early on in life and my grandmother Ruby McNeil for being my rock. In addition, to all the African American Authors who came before me thank you for being my inspiration. It is one thing to chase a dream but I also want to live it. Writing is my life, my hustle and the answer to my struggle.

Prologue

All the inmates in cellblock 5w72 stared in silence as inmate #032490 walked through the gate to enter the block. Watching him closely trying to read his facial expression, hoping he would speak on what happened at trial, but he quietly walked into his cell sat on his rack and began to write in his note pad. See he knew if he spoke on what happened, niggas would want to know every detail, so he kept quiet, ignoring the whispers of the other inmates. He began to put together everything in the cell that belonged to him but before he could finish getting his things, together one of the loudest niggas up in the block began to walk over to his cell.

He noticed two deputies coming back to the block, as they approached the block they began to call out for him but they were interrupted. "Yo, What the fuck is going on?, this dude just walked in here like forty five minutes ago quiet as hell I know this nigga got a story to tell about his trial. And now y'all walking back up in here calling his number, what's up with that I know that nigga ain't going home, no way in hell the deputies yelled loudly "inmate # 032490, you ready to go it's time". He stood up grabbed his things and walked past the inmate who wanted to know so damn much and whispered "p.o.p nigga", as he entered through the gate he had a grin on his face that was indescribable, it was as if he was just giving the key to the city or some shit. No one knew that inmate # 032490 better known as Divine Williams played his cards right and that's why he was walking out of there and them niggas were still sitting in there, wondering how he beat the system

Truly Divine Chapter 1

Divine was known around the neighborhood by the ladies as one of the smoothest brother's you ever wanted to come across, he showed a lot of female's love and affection, and the ladies had no problem showing him love right back. On the other hand, he had a well-known rep as the nigga who did not take shit from anyone. You needed something done he was the one you went to, he had a rep in the hood as the wrong nigga to fuck with, even though it was still some niggas who hated on him, and envied him no one was bold enough to take their jealousy a step further. It all started in 1990, when Divine was 15 he was hanging out in the hood with his two friends Jb and Quan, when some fake thugs came through the block from another neighborhood feeling like they had a point to prove. One of them stepped to Jb and told him to run his sneakers and his chain. Jb, who had never been in a situation like that laughed at the thugs and began to walk away, which caused the situation to escalate to the point where weapons were drawn, Divine told Jb to step back as he went in his back pack and pulled out a loaded 45. BANG, BANG, BANG. He let off three shots from his gun. He didn't think twice, "Now if you wanna leave from around here with a bullet in your throat then try me" Divine said loudly as the thugs looked at him in shock and backed off. "Aight you got it damn". They got they ass from around there quick, Divine looked at Jb and everyone standing on the block looked at Divine, and right at that moment he proved himself. Divine, Quan and Jb ran off into the building up into Jb grandmother's crib so they could sit back and cool off and clear their heads on what just happened. "Yo did you see the look on their faces, they was shook," said Quan "No did you see the look on Jb's face, I thought for sure he was going to piss on himself," said Divine with a chuckle to his voice. "Divine where you get that gun from, do your mama know you got that gun?" asked Jb "do your mama know, she need to come get your ass from around here?" said Quan as he laughed at how Jb responded to his first jacking. "Naw my mom's don't know I got this, but you better be lucky I do cause you was about to experience your first jacking, those dudes was going to have you at the court looking sick tomorrow without your sneakers, boy this is the hood not the country". They sat back laughing with each other cracking jokes and playing video games until it was time for Jb's grandmother to get in from work. "Yo I'm about to bounce I got to get my gear right for tomorrow, I'll catch up with y'all later". Divine grabbed his bags and headed down the street to his building. Once again, the elevator was broke so he had to walk up the stairs. As he reached the 4th floor he could hear a noise coming from the top stairs leading to the roof, so he quietly crept up the stairs to see where the noise was coming from, as he got closer he realized the noise was a woman moaning. Just as Divine began to peak his head around to take a closer look, a man came in from the roof door and noticed him ducking his head down, "Yo! I said Yo!" the man began yelling out to the head of what appeared to be someone who had no business up on those stairs. "Show yourself shorty" Divine stood up and looked at the guy, trying to hold a hard look on his face "yo what y'all doing up in my staircase to that woman?" Divine attempted to put a little base in his voice as he questioned the man staring at him. "Your staircase, so you own these projects lil nigga?" He asked Divine. "Naw I don't own these projects but I'm saying I live here and I feel y'all doing some disrespectful shit up in there," Divine said firmly as the man in the staircase giggled. 'Yo this lil nigga got a lot of heart talking to me like that," the man in the staircase said to the other men that were standing there looking on. The woman finished pleasing the man in the staircase. She put on her clothes and walked down the steps past Divine and gently rubbed up against his shoulder while whispering "you want some baby, thirty bucks and I can make it happen" Divine looked at her and shook his head to let her know he wasn't interested. "What you don't like women or something shorty?" the two men in the staircase asked as they stared at Divine in shock that he didn't want to take the woman up on her offer. "First of all my name isn't shorty it's Divine! and why would I give her 30 bucks to bang her up in these nasty ass stairs when I can get some from one of the girls in the hood on their mom's couch for free, I'm not paying for anything, who gave y'all niggas lessons on how to get pussy?" The men laughed at Divine. Then the man with the nice suit on said, "well first of all I'm not paying for no pussy, pussy pay me, I have customers who wanna get it so they got to pay to hit it you feel me". The man pointed to the man who came from the roof with the woman. "this dude here is a customer, that female that just left is one of my girls, I'm doing my thing I got six girls but this chick here she a beginner she got to earn her street credit first" the man walked up to Divine and asked him with a snicker in his voice "so what do you do Divine? Not sure where the conversation was going Divine answered the man question in a very sarcastic tone "Well I go to school, I play ball, chill with my boys that's about it" Divine pretty much

3

knew the answer to the question he was about to ask but he decided to ask it anyway. "So you a pimp huh, you ain't flashy at all not how they be looking on TV, big ass hats and shit slick ass hair do's'. The man giggled. "Naw I'm just me, I ain't got to be all flashy to be a smooth motherfucker, I get respect from everyone. So if you ever need something or run into something you can't handle come check me I'm not hard to find, just ask for Ace". He gave Divine a pound, telling him to be safe. As the man in the staircase began to walk away, Divine walked up the steps leading to the roof of the building and stepped out onto the roof overlooking the whole neighborhood. Standing there, he began to dwell on many things. First thing, that came to mind was the thought of making enough money to get out of the hood. He started making plans in the back of his mind. Just as he began heading down stairs to his apartment he noticed his mom walking from the elevator. "Boy, where were you?" his mother asked as she stared at him waiting for one of his famous stories pertaining to why he was never anywhere to be found. "I'm thinking you're in your room doing your homework and you hanging out somewhere". Divine knew he mother would flip if she knew he was conversing with a pimp in the staircase so he didn't bother to mention it to her. "I'm sorry ma, I ran into one of my friends that hadn't been to school in a few days so I went over to his house to go over some homework". Divine was hoping like hell his mother would accept what he told her and not ask any more questions, she believed him and walked into the kitchen to start dinner. "Well alright, you need to get your clothes ready for school and do your chores and any homework you have left because I know you didn't finish it at your friend's house; dinner will be ready in a little while". Divine did everything he had to do for the night and sat down at the table with his mom to have dinner, never once letting her know what he saw going on in the staircase. Divine, was the only child and his mother was a single mother who worked very hard to take care of him. She decided early in Divine's life that she did not want any more children. After his father walked out on her and Divine a week after his second birthday, the struggle alone was enough to help her with her decision.

****

The next day after school Divine had let Jb and Quan know what went on in the staircase. "Say word somebody was getting smashed in the hallway" Quan asked as he giggled in disbelief. "Yo she had the nerve to ask me if I wanted some, I was like hell naw, and the nigga up there was an old g nigga a pimp and shit," Divine had Quan and Jb's full attention with his crazy ass story. "Who? The nigga that was hitting it? Quan asked with a weird ass look on his face. "No! the nigga that caught me looking, shit the nigga that was hitting it ,look like that was his first time, that nigga was stuck looking all dumb in the face and shit kinda like Jb was looking yesterday". Divine said jokingly about what had happened the day earlier to Jb. they all began to bust out in laughter reminiscing on the events of yesterday, heading down to the court to play ball before the streetlights came on. Divine was always one of the flyest lil niggas on the court sporting his kicks with his matching fitted hat he knew his mother worked hard to keep him fly and he felt like it was time for him to do for himself. As the boys played around on the court Quan noticed a few girls standing courtside but they weren't paying him any attention they were too busy admiring Divine, and how well he dressed, Quan was a little jealous watching the girls blush over Divine. "Yo! We need to start working on getting some paper and I'm not talking 10 here, 15 there I'm talking bout big bills, Benjamin's and better." Quan said as he slammed the ball down. Divine knew Quan was upset because he overheard the girls whispering about Quan's shoes, Quan was always late to get the new kicks but his feet were so big he couldn't fit Divine's or Jb shoes. Divine picked up the ball and started dribbling. "Well we sure as hell ain't going to make it on the damn court all day," Divine said as he passed the ball to Jb and walked over to Quan. "So what's up Quan what are you suggesting?" Quan stood up and walked real close to Divine with a look in his eye that was very intense and said. "nigga I ain't suggesting shit I'm telling y'all niggas that I'm not going to be no little broke nigga walking around here scrambling like eggs I'm trying to get mines and keep mines and if we boys we should be seeing through the same window right about now". Jb stood up and let Quan and Divine know he was ready to get money. "Shit I'm down for whatever, y'all know grand moms be fronting on giving me allowance and shit, I gotta wait til my mom's send me money, but shit she only be sending me like 150-200 dollars, so I'm down". The boys both stared in amazement, as the one they least expected to be down for anything said he was down. "You down Jb, of all people you down for whatever, I must be dreaming" Quan said as he shook his head in disbelief. "Chill Quan damn he said he down why you trying to play him like he a punk ass nigga or something" Divine said as he tried to keep Quan calm. Divine knew Quan was trying to pick on Jb and he hated that Quan always threw the fact that Jb was a country boy in Jb's face. "Yo D this is the same one who the other day was about to let some fools roll off with his damn kicks. Shit I ain't saying he a punk ass nigga, he showed us that for himself". Jb pushed Quan upset that he was tryna play him. " Man fuck you, I ain't let them niggas punk me if that was the case I would have been running down the block crying like a little bitch kinda like you when your pops be after your ass" Jb said as he imitated Quan running down the street. Out of rage, Quan punched Jb in the face "you better watch your fucking mouth nigga! And that ain't my fucking pops" Quan said as he balled up his fist to hit Jb again. Realizing he had to do something, quick Divine intervened. "Damn chill the fuck out y'all we boys, we a fucking team and last time I checked team did not have an I in it, ain't no one better than next one, damn! Quan apologized and gave Jb a pound and they went to the court to play ball. After the game, they all decided to head home but to meet up after school, to discuss their money moves. Divine walked around the block he wasn't in a rush to get home according to his watch he still had an hour before the street lights came on. So he decided to try to find the man he met in the staircase (Ace) he passed two guys standing outside of the liquor store as he got a little closer one of their faces rung a bell in his head. "That's the dude that was getting it on with the chick in the stair case". Divine thought to himself as he walked up to the older guy to ask him if he knew where he could find Ace. "Yo anyone of you know where I can find Ace?" The two men looked at Divine as if he was begging for change. Getting annoyed by them tuning him out, he yelled "Damn! y'all can't hear I'm looking for Ace, I need to speak to him about

7

something" still no response, Divine glanced at the older men in disgust and began to walk away just then he heard a voice call out to him from the window. How may I help you shorty? Divine turned around recognizing the voice as the man in the staircase. "My name is Divine," he said firmly, Ace laughed out, "what's going on D?" He asked, signaling him to come in the building. As Divine walked into the hallway he was greeted by two women who showed him exactly which door to enter. "Damn" Divine thought to himself as he walked into the apartment, it was decked out from every angle and there was titties and ass everywhere. "What's up? Are you in trouble D?" Ace asked as he wondered what was behind Divine's visit. Divine shook his head. "Naw I just needed to talk to you about some things, because I really ain't have no one else to talk to. I'm trying to get mines and keep mine's but I want to go about it the smart way I'm not trying to get caught up, I want to do it to the fullest I don't plan to half step at all". Ace walked over to his bar and poured himself a drink he was trying to get a good understanding of what Divine plans were. "Well what is it exactly that you are trying to do? Ace asked as he took a sip of his drink. Divine looked at Ace and wondered if he was doing the right thing by talking to him about getting into the drug game, he knew this was his only chance to find out how to get started. "I'm trying to make me some money," Divine said as he looked around the room admiring the decor. Ace chuckled, he didn't know whether to take Divine serious or not. "Hell I know that, but how are you going to make that money. what is your plan, your preference, your goal? See me I specialize in women, I love women and the women love me but I also love money and if I ever have to choose between money and a bitch which one you think I'm choosing?" Divine Quickly responded "the money" Ace smiled as he patted Divine on the back. "Exactly, in this game bitches and money go hand in hand, you find the right bitch who loves money but not more than you do and you got yourself some money. The reason why I say that is because if she loves the money more than you she'll do any and everything to get it and keep it even if that means doing your ass in you hear me?" Divine agreed with Ace and continued with the convo. "I'm listening", Ace was trying to school Divine as much as possible about the game and he was glad that he had his undivided attention. "see you're still young but I can tell you got it in you to take whatever game you chose to by storm, let's just hope it's not mines" Ace said with a giggle. Respecting the knowledge as it was being giving to him, Divine let Ace know what his plans were. "I mean I like the girls and all but I don't think the pimp thing is for me" Ace knew Divine wasn't trying to take on the lifestyle as a pimp and that was cool with him he enjoyed sharing his knowledge anyway. "And it's not for everyone, some have it and some don't, some brothers couldn't make bitch sell water let alone some pussy. It's all in your words and how you use them, you can't just walk up to a girl and say hoe I want you to go over there and do this and that and bring me the money, no! It doesn't work like that. You ask the wrong one she might smack the hell out of you. to do this and do it right you must possess that thing call finesse, you take your time get to know her, find out what she likes, what she's into and then that's when you make love to her mind not her body or her heart, her mind. Once you do that, she will do anything and everything you want her to do. Ace went on and on it was as if he was teaching a

9

pimp a bitch class. "Are your parents still together, D? Ace asked.. Divine answered "No!" Wondering what did his parents being together had to do with Ace schooling him on pimping. Ace continued on "okay well look I'm going to try to give you an example the difference between a woman and a hoe. A woman wants good things, she wants her man to love her and do nice things for her and she wants to spend quality time and all that other squared out shit. A hoe ain't into all that, her main focus is to get that money, she don't have time to sit around trying to fall in love with a nigga, she is in love with the money. Divine interrupted Ace in a firm voice. "Look if pimping is your thing then it's your thing but I am not trying to be no damn pimp man no disrespect but that's not me and I'm not you, I just came over here to ask you a few questions and you're trying to school me on how to be a pimp" Ace chuckled pouring himself another drink. "Okay D, but one day that advice might come in handy, hell you don't even know what it is you want to do, so as soon as you get that all figured out come check me and I'll try to help you the best way I can". Divine looked down at his watch and noticed he had ten minutes to get home. Damn I gotta go but I am going to think about my plan and I will come back another day to talk to you about it." Divine walked out of the door and headed home thinking about everything the old g was saying to him. When Divine got in his mom was already preparing dinner so he went ahead and started on his homework and followed his normal routine, did his chores and took his shower. Sitting at the table Divine's mom stared at him without saying a word she just looked at her son praying to herself that he wouldn't be anything like his father who had walked out on her and never showed his face since. "Are you okay Divine?" his mother asked. Divine looked at his mom's face and could tell she had something on her mind. "I'm fine just thinking about this test I have for tomorrow in my math class". Divine didn't have a test coming up but he knew he couldn't sit in his mother's face under her roof and tell her what he really was thinking about. Happy to hear her son was focused on schoolwork she smiled "well don't worry yourself too much just study hard and I'm sure you'll pass". She kissed him on the forehead as she walked towards the sink to start on the dishes, Divine told his mother good night and went into his room to get ready for his day ahead of him and to focus on his plans of getting money. The next day Divine let Quan and Jb know where he went yesterday "y'all know I didn't go straight home yesterday" he said cheesing, "where you went on a coochie chase?" Quan asked as he laughed out Divine punched Quan in the shoulder "nigga you know I don't chase no coochie, coochie chase me, naw remember that old nigga I told y'all about, the one from the stair case? He asked to see if Jb and Quan remembered the man from his crazy ass story. They both nodded their heads letting him know they did. "Well I went to go talk to him yesterday about how to get it and keep it and this nigga sitting up in the crib trying to school me on how to be a pimp and on top of that he had titties and ass everywhere and I do mean everywhere. But I told him that's not me, that's not my thing". Quan couldn't believe Divine turned that offer down. "Let me get this straight that nigga a pimp and he had a crib full of titties and ass and tried to get you to be a pimp and you turned him down. nigga is you crazy?, Hell he probably would have started you out with two of his best girls right then and there and you talking bout naw, nigga where he stay at hell I'll pimp a hoe, and love it too. You get to tell them what to do all day every day and get paid for it, you dumb as hell". Quan said as he bragged on about how he would be the best pimp in the world. Divine made it clear pimping just wasn't his thing. " I ain't being no pimp and neither are you come on that's for them old niggas shit we can do anything we want and we going to get this money and we not going to half step with it. We are going to get in the game the drug game". Quan and Jb stared at him with confusion. Divine continued on "we not going to come into the game owing anybody shit y'all hear me? We going to walk into this shit with our own" Divine was very precise with his decision "and just where the hell are we going to get the money to do all that?" Quan asked wondering how they were going to get into the game without any money. Divine looked at Quan and Jb without a blink in his eye. "Well if it means saving our allowance or sacrificing a pair of fresh kicks then so be it". Just then, Jb came up with an idea "yo! We can sell candy" "what!" asked Quan " how the hell do you figure selling candy will get us in the drug game" Quan starts laughing refusing to take Jb serious. Annoyed by Quan's laughter Jb interrupts. "Well if you let me finish I'll tell you. Y'all know how my grand mom's works up in that store downtown well they be having everything up in there and I can make up something to see if she could get us some boxes of candy to sell. So whatever we make we can put into our lil bank. I will tell her we are trying to start our own basketball team in the park but we need money to get the shirts. You know I'm about to game the hell outta grandma" Jb said putting his hand up to get a high five from Divine and Quan. "We'll see nigga, we'll see" Quan said with a giggle, he patted Jb on the back, he wasn't really with the selling candy thing but he had no other choice. he knew he couldn't get the money from his mother hell she had six other children in the house, including him and the only time that household saw any money is on the 1st or the 15th or if mom's got lucky with the numbers. Divine wasn't completely feeling Jb's idea but he figured it was worth a try. "So Jb see if your grandmother is going to buy your story about our fake ass basketball team and we'll meet up tomorrow after school same place same time" said Divine as he gave Jb a pound. The three of them walked away from the park that night with a different look in their eyes, the look of Motivation, and deep down each one knew the other's reason for wanting to go through with this plan, so no one complained and no one backed out each one was down. Later that night Jb waited til after dinnertime to ask his grandmother about the candy, he never really asked her for anything so she figured it was one of his friends putting him up to it. "What do you and your friends need all that candy for?" She asked with her hand on her hip. Not sure if she would believe his reason for needed a few boxes of candy but he knew he would get clowned if he showed up at the park tomorrow without any good news. "Well we've been playing ball down at the park and we thought it would be cool if we started our own little team and got matching outfits and some other things". Jb said with slight hesitation. Seeing the look on her grandson's face his grandmother smiled with pride, agreed to help him, and said. "Well that sounds like a plan, I'll see what I can do, I tell you what I'll get the candy for you guys on one condition". Jb wasn't sure what the condition was so he asked. "What's that?" she smiled and replied. "Every Sunday after church you boys come down and help out and who knows I may be able to talk some of my fellow church goers into buying some candy as well. Jb knew he couldn't tell his grandmother no and still expect her to get the candy but he knew telling her yes without talking to the other first was going to cause some drama. "We'll do it," he said even though he knew when Divine and Quan found out they were going to be upset. Jb's grandmother hugged him and said, "Then it's settled every Friday I will get you guy's six boxes of candy each. Jb walked into his room trying to add up the amount of boxes multiplied by the three of them. "Wow that's a lot of candy," he thought to himself, as he got ready for the next day. Jb's grandmother was happy to know that her grandson was trying to do something positive other than stand on the corner all day like some of the kids she passed by on her way to and from work. The next day Quan and Divine were eager to hear what Jb's grandmother had to say, little did they know they were in for a big surprise. Jb walked up with a big Kool-Aid smile on his face. "Okay I got some good news and I got some bad news which one do y'all want to hear first?" he asked as Divine and Quan eagerly waited to hear what his grandmother had to say. "Let me guess grand mom's told you no!" said Quan as he sucked his teeth, "Nope" replied Jb "what's up Jb what she say" asked Divine, "well grandma bought the basketball story and she'll get us the candy but we have to help out down at the church every Sunday". Quan and Divine responded at the same time "WHAT! What you mean we? Nigga you asked her that was your bright idea". Said Quan as he stomped his feet with anger. "Yeah and it's going to help all three of us!" Jb said as he tried to convince Quan and Divine helping grandma would be worth it. Uninterested by helping out at church Quan starts to flip out. "All that mess you was talking yesterday" Quan shakes his head as he begins to imitate Jb. "I'm about to game the hell outta grandma. Looks like grandma gamed the hell outta you and us too" Divine and Jb bust out in laughter. "Damn Jb she got us" said Divine. "OH well did she say how much candy she would get for us?" asked Quan. "Six boxes each and in each box is about fifty pieces of candy," replied Jb. The three of them sat on the bench and tried to calculate their future earnings. Divine pulled out a pen and said "ok let's add this shit up six boxes multiplied by three gives us eighteen, multiplied by fifty gives us nine hundred, nine hundred multiplied by one dollar gives us?" Divine stopped to look over his mathematics making sure what he was looking at on paper was correct.

"Way more than what my mom's sends me" said Jb with the look of money in his eyes. Looking at the total on paper and knowing that was his only way to get money and a few things for himself; Quan agreed. "Yo! Jb it's all good, for that right there I'll help out at the church". Said Quan, as he high fived Jb. So that was it, their plan was to sell candy, save allowances, make sacrifices whatever it took to get them started. each one wrote down a list of neighborhoods that they figured would be good places to sell their candy at, and on Sunday's they would go down and help Jb's grandmother clean up after church and sell candy to them old ladies too. "Yo Quan you think your mom's will let you stay the night out? Asked Divine, he wanted to make sure their candy-selling plan started smooth. He wanted them to get an early start. Quan wasn't sure his mother had any plans; he knew if she did, he would be stuck in the house. "I don't know, why" asked Quan "duh," replied Divine "because today is Friday, which means when Jb's grandmother get's home she's going to have the candy, and if we're already at his house we can get up and start early on our candy runs". Quan agreed and decided to check with his mother about him spending the night out. As he walked towards the front door to his building, he signaled them to wait for him. "Hold up let me run to the house and ask my mom's, hopefully she'll be in a good mood, and let a nigga have a night out". Quan says as he heads to his building while Divine and Jb wait at the park for him. Divine looks at his watch " damn I need to go in the house and call my mom's and ask if I can chill at your house, which I'm sure she'll say yes I ain't got shit else to do, I hope that nigga, Quan mom's say it's alright she be tripping". Divine said as he wondered if Quan would be able to get out the house. "Damn she mean like that"? Asked Jb. Divine looked over at Jb realizing he never been in Quan's house, he tells him about the time he saw for himself how Quan's mother be tripping. "That's right you ain't never met his mom's, well she's not mean like that but he's the oldest and she be getting on him and shit about everything. A while back, I had stopped over there to meet him before school and he was talking bout he wasn't going because he had to baby-sit for his mom's she had an appointment down town. Feeling bad for Quan, Jb says "damn she couldn't get no babysitter, that's gotta suck sitting in the house stuck with some bad ass kids. Just then Quan walks up, "what y'all niggas out here?" he asked as he peeped Jb and Divine laughing "Talking about you nigga, we thought mom dukes was going to say hell no you can't go" Divine said as he imitated Quan's mother voice. "naw not this time she gave a nigga a get outta jail free card, I told her we were helping Jb grandmother out this weekend at the church so I don't have to be back til Sunday by seven"

Quan said happy as hell that his mother allowed him to get out of the house and live a little. "Damn and she fell for that, I hope she don't be calling my grandmother phone all night" Jb said as he hoped Quan's mother wouldn't make it her business to get proof of Quan's little story. "Naw she cool she know your grandmother and she respect her she wouldn't do no shit like that" Quan said assuring Jb he had nothing to worry about. They headed to Divine's building. "Y'all coming up stairs?" Divine asked as he started to head up to his apartment. Quan and Jb nodded their head yes, as they walked into the building and got on the elevator. As they were coming onto the floor, "yo is this the stair case right here?" Quan asked looking around as if he was hoping to see some more action taken place. "Damn you still thinking about that shit I told you?" asked Divine as he responded to Quan's question. "Yeah that's the staircase but come on so I can call my mom before she leaves work". Divine calls his mom and gets her permission to stay out for the weekend at Jb's house while Quan and Jb look around the living room. "Yo! This crib is banging as hell if I ain't come through the building I would not think we were in the projects. Says Jb as he admired the way Divine house was hooked up. Divine appreciates the compliment and tells Jb a little about his mother. "My mom's is into all that fashion shit, the latest this, the latest that, she does her thing, we alright. Yo, y'all ready. Let me grab my stuff and we can be out". They head out the door before they get to the elevator they notice an older man walking towards Divine's door. "May I help you with something? Divine asks as he turns away from the direction of the elevator, looking at the man as if he seen him somewhere before. He couldn't match the face with a place, just then the older man asked him if a woman by the name of Denise lived there. "No woman by the name of Denise lives at this apartment". Said Divine as he headed back towards the elevator, Quan and Jb didn't really know why Divine lied to the man about his mother living there but they figured he had his reasons. The older man walked down the stairs as Divine, Jb and Quan got on the elevator. "Who the fuck was that dude?" asked Quan, "and why did you tell him your mom didn't live there?"Jb and Quan both wanted answers. Divine looked a little upset and replied, "Something did not seem right with that nigga and since I'm not going to be home for a couple of days, I don't need any nigga lurking around and shit. I mean my moms can handle herself but I don't trust niggas I don't know". They headed to Jb's building to put their plan in motion.

Let the Hustle Begin chapter 2

It was Saturday morning; the smell of breakfast woke the boy's right up, Quan hadn't smelled cooking like that in a long time, his mother was too busy running the streets to make breakfast. "Damn Jb your grand mom's up making breakfast". Said Quan, he enjoyed the aroma in the house. "Yep, and I'm about to go get some too" said Jb while he stretched. As they got up to get themselves together, they noticed eighteen boxes of candy on the floor. "grand moms wasn't playing at all, you see all that damn candy" said Divine as his eyes lit up looking at all the different candy boxes on the bedroom floor, just then Jb's grandmother walked in with a cheery voice. "Good morning guys, I made you some breakfast so you can get ready for your first day at selling all this candy", they each said thank you as they grabbed their toothbrushes and wash cloths. Jb's grandmother reminded them of their holy obligation as she headed out of the room. "I want to see y'all down at the church around 3 p.m.". Her words stopped them dead in their tracks. "Damn" they whispered   Jb knew he had to say something before their silence made his grandmother change her mind. "We'll be there," he yelled from the room as Divine and Quan snickered. Everyone was Dressed and ready to go; they grabbed up some boxes and headed out of the door stopping at every hair salon, playground, train station, bus stop anywhere they knew they could get a buck for a candy bar. By then end of the night that had got rid of six boxes and they were shocked their first day went so good. "Damn six down and twelve more to go" said Divine as he applauded their progress. "Nobody said selling candy would make you this tired my

19

feet hurt," said Quan as he looked down at his sneakers. Mentally prepared to sell some more candy Divine says, "We still got tomorrow before church" the three of them headed back to Jb's apartment to get ready for tomorrow.

****

Sunday morning was here, there was no smell of breakfast cooking because Jb's grandmother had left out for early service.so everyone was on they own for breakfast. Once that was outta the way they grabbed their boxes of candy and headed out the door. "I know we are not going to go to the same places we went yesterday," asked Quan, he wasn't too intrigued by the thought of all that walking around. "No we're going to Whiteyville," said Divine "Whiteyville?" Jb wanted to know where exactly was Whiteyville, because he had never heard of that place before; Whiteyville was the term for the white neighborhood and Divine knew going there would most likely get all the candy sold and maybe even at a higher price depending on the buyer. Divine looked down at the boxes of candy and smiled. "Yeah, Whiteyville we're going out there to see if we can get this done quicker, you know we find enough fat people out there we just might get lucky" said Divine as he joke on how much money they would make if they saw the right fat people. They all began to laugh as Divine continued on with his reasons for wanting to go to Whiteyville. Looking down at his sneakers and knowing he wasn't prepared for any long walks Quan stops Divine and asks, "Well how are we getting there? I know we are not walking" Divine looks at Quan amused that he would even think they were going to walk all the way there. "Hell no we not walking we're taking the train, well actually we're taking about three trains get up there get back and still make it to church to help out", Divine said as he shared he travel plans with Quan and Jb. they headed to the train station, while waiting for the train, they noticed they were being watched. Nevertheless, that didn't keep them from clowning around in the station. As their train was entering the station, they were getting ready to get on, the man notices they have candy and yells out to them. "Bingo" Divine thought to himself as he turns to walk toward the man, who showed interest in the boxes they were holding. "You guys selling candy or something? The man asked with a look of hunger on his face. Shaking his head about the dumb ass question, he just heard, he replies sarcastically. "Yeah we're selling candy, why you want to buy some" the man's eyes lit up as he reached for his wallet. "Yeah let me get six bars," he says as he checks his currency, looking in on in disbelief that the man wanted that much candy Quan blurted out. "Six bars! Damn" Divine hits Quan on the arm to signal him to let him handle the candy deal. "Shut up, Quan if the man wants six bars he'll get six bars" Divine says as he pulls the candy bars from the box and hands them to the eagerly waiting man. "That will be six dollars," say Divine waiting for the man to give him the money. The man pulls out six dollars and hands it to the Divine, while grabbing the candy bars noticing the boys looking at the map of the subway, he asks, "you guys ain't from around here are you?" damn was it that obvious Divine thinks to himself and replies. "No! We are just trying to find a few good places to sell our candy, so that we can get new uniforms and equipment for our basketball team. do you know where we can go around here? the man points to a area on a map in the train station letting them know where a few parks are so they could sell the most candy. "Thanks man" Divine says as he walks back over to Quan and Jb and let them know what train they needed to take. "Good luck you guys," the man yells out as he heads in the opposite direction. Once on the train, Quan starts wondering why Divine didn't over charge the man he Questions the transaction while scratching his head. "Damn D, why you didn't charge him extra, shit you should have made that nigga pay like he weigh" Quan says chuckling, Divine agrees. "I know right, but he was already getting six bars and how we just get out here and start gypping niggas, y'all see he showed us where we could go, now had I charged him more than that we probably be standing back there looking stupid. Come on, this our stop let's go get rid of this candy". Once outside they find the area that the man told them about and they make their rounds, just their luck there was some type of game going on at a field they were passing by. Dollars signs fill Divine eyes as he looks at Jb and Qaun. "Are you niggas thinking what I'm thinking? They both respond in unison. "Yes we are". They walk over to the field and stand by the fence pretending to watch the game hoping someone will walk up to them and ask about the candy. Once again, Quan had complaints. "I know we are not about to stand here all day? he asked as he impatiently waited to make a sell. "No we're not, Quan but we're not going to just come out and say, "hey wanna buy some candy! Let them come to us". Divine said as he assured his friends they were going to make some money. "Hey Jb what do you want to do?" asked Divine. Thinking about the promise they had made to his grandmother and how disappointed she would be if they didn't show up, he said, "I know I don't want to get back too late or we are going to hear it from my grandmother, so why don't we either say something or leave". Before they could make a pitch to sell their candy they noticed the game was over and everyone on the field was packing up but there were a few kids that noticed them standing by the fence, so they walked over and asked the three of them what they were doing around there. Quan quickly responded, "We're selling candy, why you want to buy some?" One white kid eyes lit up and said, "Hold up I'll run over there and get some money from my dad and I'll be right back". The white kid runs over and comes back with twenty dollars how much can I get with this and holds out a twenty-dollar bill. Surprised at the fact, the kid was trying to get as much candy as he could with twenty dollars. "your father gave you twenty dollars for some candy" asked Divine the kid shook his head and replied " he'll give me anything I want as long as I don't go to live with my mom, but that's a long story y'all going to give me the candy or what?" Divine pulled out the candy bars, "Well for twenty dollars, you will get ten candy bars. What's your name?" The white kid responded in a very proper tone. "My name is Jeremiah" "Jeremiah! What kind of name is that?" Quan asks as he busts out in laughter. Divine looks at Quan and tries hard not to join in on the laughter and reaches out to give the white kid a pound. "Well Jeremiah, my name is Divine, that's Jb and the clown over there is Quan. We would stay and conversate but it looks like your father is waiting for you and we need to go, you got a number or something? You know just in case we're ever around here again and want to hang out with you". Jeremiah gave the boys his number and ran over to his father to leave the field, his father stared at Quan, Divine and Jb as if he was wondering what his son was doing talking to them. "What's up with the white boy D, you trying to be cool with him or something asking for numbers and shit?" Quan asked because he never knew Divine to hang out with any white kids. Divine knew what he was doing and he responded with confidence. "He just bought ten candy bars and he look like he can get money anytime he want it from his father so he might come in handy one day. As they headed back towards the train they realized they had sold all of their candy except for five bars, they made it back to their neighborhood in just enough time to get to the church to help Mrs. Jenkins. While helping at church Quan wanted to really know why Divine was being so quiet he whispered to Jb "Jb what's up with D, he hasn't really said anything since we've been here, and I'm still trying to figure out why he asked the white boy for his number?" Jb knew Quan was extremely skeptical by his questioning Divine's actions, he didn't have a problem with what Divine had done, he looked at Quan and replied. "Divine did say he might come in handy Quan why are you so worried about it, I mean we're all boys we tight I doubt D is planning to up and bounce on us to go hang out with the white boy" Divine overheard them and jumped in the conversation, " white boy who Jeremiah? Divine looked at Quan and said wow, you're still thinking about that, damn I told you that he might come in handy one day and that's it I don't know why you're still dwelling on it". Quan's facial expression made it clear he wasn't buying Divine's lame response. "I really don't see how you feel he could come in handy cause he bought some damn candy bars, if that's the case then the fat nigga who bought some on the train can come in handy". Quan said as he mocked Divine's decision. Upset by the mockery Divine stepped to Quan's face. "you know what Quan that's your problem you never try to look towards the future you sitting here talking about candy bars, I'm thinking about something totally different stop being so fucking hot headed for once and just trust me on this". Divine said, as he was growing tired of explaining his decision. They finished cleaning around the church and headed back to the block, Divine and Jb chilled at Divine's house while Quan headed home.

****

The weeks went by fast and before they knew it they had been selling candy non-stop for a month, When they were done they went to Divine's house to count everything they saved. Divine pulled out his calculator and began to start count. "Aight Quan before we count the candy money what you got?" Divine asked as he started punching number in the calculator. Quan reached in his pockets and pulled out some crumbled up bills. "Shit all I got is 30 Dollars, how bout you Jb?" Quan asks as he looks over at Jb. "Let's see the 20.00 my grandmother' gives me every week outta the money my Mom sends so I got about 80.00, what you working with over there D?" Jb asked as he placed his money on the bed. Divine started counting his cash. "I got my allowance every week and I stashed it, so that's 100.00," said Divine as he continued to add up their funds. Finishing his count, he let them how much money they made. "okay plus the money we got from the candy, we looking at 3,810.00" excited by the total Quan jumped up and yelled out, "damn yo we did it, we really did it!" Divine joined in on the excitement "hell yeah we did it now we bout to get it fo'real, no one would have ever believed three little niggas from the projects came up in the game by selling candy", they gave each other a pound. Wondering what their next move was, Quan asked Divine what his plans were. "So D what are we going to do now? I mean we should have enough to get something right, yo! My mom said we're supposed to be visiting my aunt in Philly and I have some cousins out there who always be smoking weed and shit I can ask them what's up". Semi-interested in what Quan was speaking about Divine responded to Quan. "So your cousin is a pot head and you think he is really going to tell you where you can get some weed from, yeah ok nigga they going to laugh at your ass or try to rob you". Divine said as he laughed at Quan's idea. Quan was quick to let Divine and Jb know he wasn't no fool, "rob who? You think I'm dumb enough to take money up there hell no, I'm just going to ask him that's all". Divine nodded his head and agreed with the plan. "Aight bet, when you go up there just talk don't let that nigga know all our business I know he your family but shit y'all ain't close like that and if he talking good see when we can go up there or he can come down here and do business". Quan was happy Divine was taking him seriously. "That's cool I will do that, we're leaving this weekend".

****

The weekend came and Quan had left with his mom to go to Philly. Divine stopped over to Jb's house to see had he heard from Quan. "What's up Jb, you talked to Quan?" Jb shook his head no, "Naw D, I hope he ain't get up there and forget about what he was supposed to check on" said Jb Divine agreed but knew they might have to go a different route. " well if that don't work I have something else in mind" said Divine as he thought about going back to Ace's crib and getting some information from him, just then there was a knock on the door. Jb looked through the peephole excited to see Quan on the other side of the door. "Speaking of the devil, what's up? Quan, damn we thought you forgot about our plans." Said Jb as he let Quan in the house making sure it was ok to speak freely about their plans to get money Quan asked Jb if his grand mom's home. "Naw she's at the church why? Asked Jb Quan felt comfortable knowing they were the only was in the apartment broke down the situation to them. "Because my cousin is here, he drove me down here; you know so we can talk about that thing, he's in the hallway is it ok if he comes inside?" Jb and Divine let Quan know it was ok for him to bring his cousin into the apartment so he opened the door and signaled him to come in. "yo cuz these are my boys D and Jb and homies this is my cousin Raymond". They dapped each other up and proceeded to talk about their money-making moves Divine decided to speak first "What's up? Did your cousin tell you what it is we are trying to do? Raymond let him know Quan shared their lil plan with him. "Yeah he told me, but before we get into that I need to know y'all serious about this shit, cause I'm not with the games and I roll with the big dogs. I don't get down for the little kiddie bullshit". Raymond said firmly, Divine could tell Raymond meant business. But he wanted him to know they meant business as well. "No disrespect but we bout the realest niggas you going to see around here and we ain't for the bullshit neither". Divine said as he tried to keep a mean mug. The four of the sat down at the table politicked for a minute, then Raymond & Quan took the money and rode back to Philly , Divine and Jb chilled in the crib until they heard from Quan. later that night Quan called them to let them know everything would be ready by tomorrow so Divine decided to head home and that they would meet back at Jb's crib since his grandmother would be at church another night. The next day Jb, D and Quan met up, Quan told them Raymond would be arriving within the next thirty minutes. Once Raymond arrived he honked the horn and let them know to meet him down stairs, he handed them each three grocery bags of what appeared to be boxes of cereal. They went back to Jb's crib opened up the boxes and realized it was far from corn flakes in the boxes. The strong smell of marijuana hit their noses hard. Divine pulled a few pieces out "damn that nigga Raymond a smooth mother fucker, I like his style, Putting this shit in the cereal boxes". Divine was liking the situation already, Jb was a little nervous he never sold drugs before and he knew it was a little different from selling candy bars with a lost look on his face he asked. "Okay now what's up what are we going to do?" Confident they had just made a wise choice Divine smiled and said. "First thing first every crew needs a name, let's go with G.M.C". The initials were a no brainer for Quan so he agreed right away. Jb, on the other hand was a little thrown off by the initials, he looked at Divine with a confused look on his face uttering the initials "G. M.C?" Divine laughed and broke it down to his friend. "Yeah Getting Money Crew, now we need some pagers and we need to put this in something so when niggas see it they know it's us. Quan made a suggestion, "let's go to the spot on Beverly ave and get some bags from there" Divine shook his head "naw I don't want no shit everybody got, let's get some plain bags and put our own symbol on it". Quan agreed "yeah that sounds cool, we can go downtown to get the pagers they got some banging ones at this store next to the tattoo spot". So it was done, the getting money crew was getting that money. They had decided that their symbol on their bags would be a dollar sign surrounded by flames, they were doing their thing on a regular basis, being very careful not to get caught by anyone. they went down to the mall and got the latest style kicks to match the t- shirts they had made, along with their hat's and bandana's g. m. c was starting to be a well known name around the neighborhood. One day Jb's grandmother questioned him about his logo on his shirt. "Let me guess good motivated Christians". She said with smile on her face. Jb looked at his grandmother almost forgetting the candy-selling story but quickly caught himself before he responded. "No, grandma it stands gracefully moving crowds because that's what we do when we're on the court everyone knows our name and they cheer for us". Jb could see the smile on his grandmother's face but didn't want to get her too excited because she might offer to take off of work one day to watch him play. So he kept his story very short.

****

Time had passed and now g. m. c was two years into the game everything was looking lovely for them, no complaints at all. Quan had moved out of his mother's house and was staying with Divine. They had grew up they loved the game but they wanted more. Divine's mom was barely home, she took up some night classes so by the time she came in Divine was either sleep or out with his friends. Denise never questioned her son about anything that he was doing, the clothing, the pager nothing made her think twice about what her son was out there doing, she just figured he was a teenager and getting into the parties, the girls and so on and so forth. She did make it very clear to Quan that she didn't want no fast ass girls up in her house and she didn't want no one's mama coming to her house or calling her phone talking bout her son or his friend got their daughter pregnant and she sure as hell didn't want the cops coming to her house. They understood the rules and they respected them even though they would still have girls in the crib they made sure they strapped up and didn't leave any wrappers laying around the house. Jb was still living at his grandmother's he had been a little distant for the past two months because his grandmother was very sick and he had been going back and forth with her to the doctor. His mother had come to visit but she didn't stay long. She was too much in a rush to get back to her new husband, whom Jb didn't like very much. Jb knew there was no way in hell he was going to move back home with her if something did happened with his grandmother, even though his mother promised him that once she got on her feet that she was going to send for him. That day never came, she ended up getting married and forgetting the promise, she made to her son and her mother. Mrs. Jenkins had got very sick so the doctor requested that she be admitted to the hospital, a week after being admitted, Mrs. Jenkins passed away. Jb took it very hard the first few days but he knew that he had to be strong and now all he had was his boys to count on. At the funeral, everyone from the church and Mrs. Jenkins job had come to pay his or her respects. The pastor let Jb know that he was very proud of how he was handling himself and how much of a good job he did preparing for the funeral. No one questioned him on where he got the money from; they assumed his grandmother's life insurance covered everything. Divine could see that Jb was holding in his tears in front of everyone so he walked over to comfort his friend. "Are you alright JB, he knew Jb wasn't ok as long as he knew him he's always been with his grandmother, Jb lifted his head up and responded to his friend. "Man I'm holding up as good as I'm going to", looking around and noticing Jb's mother wasn't there Divine shook his head in disbelief. "Damn, I can't believe your mother did not come". Jb got upset as he talked about his mother not being there. "Man fuck her, she thinks because she sent some flowers and shit that it's okay if she didn't come. I am glad she didn't show her face here my grandmother probably would have got up out of her casket and smacked the hell outta her. Wanting to know what Jb, plans were pertaining to his living arrangements so what you going to do about the apartment. Jb looked at Divine and told him what he decided, "I'm going to live here nigga as a matter of fact I have a plan" wanting to know what Jb was thinking about he asked curiously. "What's your master plan Jb? Jb smiled and said, "how about we all move up in the crib that way we can handle our business all in one spot" Quan overheard his friends plans and joined in on the conversation. "No disrespect, Jb but I'm not too comfortable living up in no dead person's crib" Quan said shaking his head. Divine actually thought the plan was a good one and tried to convince Quan to agree. "damn Quan you act like she died in the house, she died in the hospital, I mean Jb has a point besides its way more room to roam at his crib" Quan agreed and Jb stood up and gave him a pound. "So it's a deal; you guys just come sometime tomorrow" Jb said his goodnight's to everyone that came over and Divine and Quan went to pack all of their belongings. The next day they headed over to their new spot, as they were leaving Divine noticed his mom walking up the street. He approached her and let her know his plans, she warned her son to be careful because the streets were nothing to play with. She had done all she could do, her first-born son wasn't a baby anymore; he was growing up and starting to live his own life. She wasn't going to scold him with the things her mother scolded her about; staying in school, graduating, going to college. she could look at her son and could tell that it would have went in one ear and right out the other, Denise watched carefully as her son walked down the street, then she headed into the building she knew he wasn't too far if he needed her or she needed him. Later that night Divine and Quan helped Jb fix up the crib to make it a little bit more comfortable for them. After they were finished, they sat down and begin to bag up some more work for the next day. Pulling out a stack of 1oo dollar bills and placing it on the table. "Damn this money is good but we can't sell this shit forever, do y'all know how much money we could see if we got our hands on some other shit, Quan said trying to convince the crew they could make major paper. " like what nigga? Crack, cocaine, heroin" Divine wanted to know what Quan was suggesting. Quan pulled out a bag of weed and said, "anything but this nigga, I'm trying to get it and keep it ain't that what you're always saying D? Divine agreed with Quan. "I hear you loud and clear Quan, let me think shit over and I'm going to give you with an answer in the morning". Divine mentally made his decision before he went to sleep and he knew exactly where he would go. That morning Divine woke up early and left the house before Quan and Jb woke up, he went to go check on an old friend, he hadn't seen Ace in a while, he had questions, and he knew Ace would have answers. As he got to the block, he noticed a few things had changed; there were different curtains in the window, the different appearance almost made him turn away but just then as always Ace noticed him walking up and called out, "yo D where you been at? Come on up". Divine walked into the building this time there was no titties and ass to greet him just the sound of the door unlocking. Ace, invited him in and complimented him on his come up in the game. "Long time, no see D what's been going on? You look like life has been treating you good. Real good" Divine smiled as he entered the apartment. With a humble tone "well it can always be better and I'm working on that now. I came to talk to you about some real shit, I've been doing my thing in the game but I'm trying to go one step further I'm trying to get my hands on that powder that chyna white". Divine didn't have to spell it out because Ace knew exactly what he was talking about. However, he wanted to make sure Divine was ready to get into the coke game. "Well D, you know I have connections when it comes to that. Are you sure, you are ready for that kind of hustle. Can you and your team handle that much money and that much clientele? Coke is a very fast-paced drug. Divine pulled out his chrome.45 on the table and looked over at Ace. "I'm ready for anything, I wouldn't be approaching you with this if I wasn't" then he popped open his box of money. Ace looked at box full of cash impressed by what he saw. "Damn not only did you come determined you came prepared I like that, well look let me get these dudes on the phone to arrange a little meeting and get the ball rolling. But I'm warning you these dudes they don't play at all, they are very serious dudes and dangerous too. So make sure you stay on top of your shit when you dealing with them. Ace warned Divine and he took the warning serious. "Oh I got this under control, you just handle that for me and I got you. You always kept it real with me Ace, so I'm not going to forget that or go against that". Divine said as he proceeded to leave the apartment. He noticed the whole time he was sitting there he didn't see any females walk in or out. "Where are the ladies at tonight? I didn't see no titties or ass the whole time I was sitting here he laughed as he looked around the room. Ace chuckled "my ladies are out of town doing some very interesting things, but they'll be back soon with all my money too." Divine shook his head as he agreed with Ace. "I like that you still pimping them hoes, well we're having a party this weekend if they're back send them through and they will get paid trust me. Divine said as he gave Ace a pound and headed back to the crib to let Quan and Jb know that everything was in the works for them to start getting that major paper. After Divine, left Ace made a few phone calls and everything was set. Quan hears Divine walking in the door "damn nigga where was you at? Asks Quan since Divine hadn't been in the house all day. "I went to check on that thing we talked about and get some girls for the party this weekend, what y'all niggas doing? Asks Divine as he sat on the sofa. "Shit we got rid of the rest of that work, so now we waiting to get that other shit out there. Jb said he would go check Raymond and get some more of that good plant for the block and the party". Quan was super hype, next to making money he loved to party and flash his cash. Hinting that things were about to take a turn for the better divine let Jb know there was no need to overdo the order. "Yo! Jb just get enough of that shit don't go overboard cause by tomorrow we should have our order in, then we can pass this shit on to the little niggas". Understanding what Divine was saying without him saying it Jb agreed. "Yeah D I feel you I just put the order in with Raymond cause we ain't know if we were gonna make major moves or not, we gotta stay on top of our game. Divine got a confirmation from Ace that his order would be ready in the morning. Everything was going as planned Ace took care of the order. Divine , Quan and Jb were getting ready for their party, they had the hood going crazy, they were hated and loved at the same time by the bitches, niggas and the fiends, Money was looking good for the three of them, they hit the block like clockwork never missed a beat.

Time to Make Moves Chapter 3

It was getting closer to the big 21 for the members of the G.M.C crew their party was in a few days they planned to do it up, hood style as they sat around in the crib; Divine began to speak about that time they went to Whiteyville to sell candy. "Yo remember when we were selling candy and we met that white boy, damn what was his name" Divine was trying to think back to the day and the conversation to remember the name the white boy gave him. Finally, the name came to mind. "Jeremiah, yeah that's right Jeremiah I wonder what ever happened with his ass, as a matter of fact I think I still have that number he gave me". Divine searched through his box in his closet and found the number without hesitation he called; a woman with an accent answered the phone "hello", hoping he has the right number he asks to speak to Jeremiah. The woman on the other end tells Divine to hold on and takes the telephone to Jeremiah; he greets the caller not knowing who was on the other end. "Hello, this is Jeremiah, who am I speaking to? He asks as the voice on the other end of the phone begins to speak. "I'm not sure if you remember me but we met a while back in Whiteyville my bad I meant in your neighborhood I sold you some candy". Divine catches himself before he offends Jeremiah. Remembering that day as if it was yesterday because his father scolded him, for talking to kids, he didn't know. "Yeah, the candy boy, what was your name again? He asked Divine, knowing the white kid probably forgot his name as soon as he walked away on the field that day he reminded him, that his name was Divine but he could call him D. Jeremiah was happy to hear from Divine he had

36

always wondered why the kid who sold him candy never returned to his neighborhood. "Wow it's been a long time since that day I bought that candy. Divine agreed. "Yeah it sure has been a long time; well I was wondering what was up with you and possibly invite you to a little party. Those were drinking words for Jeremiah, filled with excitement he said. "a party, hell yeah anything to get from around here my dad's been riding me about colleges and other shit I don't want to hear Jeremiah got Divine's party location and number and confirmed he would be there. Divine had money on the brain as usual; as he hung up the phone, Quan had questions as usual. "What was that about? Divine looked at Quan with a grin. "Business, just business" not clear as to what business had to do with him inviting the white boy Quan continued probing. "I'm not following, so please explain why the fuck you just invited this white dude to our party? Divine decided to explain his reasons for the invite. "Well I figure our boy Jeremiah could get us in the door with a few of his white friends, I'm sure a few of them wouldn't mind doing a few lines trust me on this". Quan wasn't comfortable at all with Divine's decision but he got off the subject and headed out to grab some gear for the party.

****

Friday night came and the crib was decked out. Filled with everything a nigga in the hood would want; drinks, smoke, hoes and coke. Ace had sent over eight of his thickest finest females true moneymakers. The ones that a made a nigga cum in his pants just by bending over. A few hours into the party, a B.M.W. pulled up in front of the building, looking totally out of place. Jeremiah hopped out of the car, Quan noticed a few thugs getting ready to give him a welcome to the hood beat down. Calling out to divine to go and help his boy. "Yo D I think your boy is downstairs and you better go help him get up stairs", Divine looked out the window and noticed Jeremiah was looking nervous as hell. He yelled out the window "Yo! J, up here 4th floor, get on the elevator stay away from the stairs. When the thugs heard Divine's, voice the backed, off. Divine called out to one of the local big bodies on the block. "Yo! Homeboy" he yelled pointing to Jeremiah's car. "You see that ride don't let anyone touch that shit don't even let them breathe on It." After hearing Divine's request none was going to even look at that car let alone touch it. Once upstairs, Jeremiah was greeted by two seductively dressed females. "Hey Baby! Filled with lust and on a money prowl they both wanted to fuck the white guy who just pulled up in the B.M.W. Caught in a trance as he gazed at their overly exposed breasts, Jeremiah said hello. Divine could see that the women were about to get them some easy cash before he could really kick it with Jeremiah, he rushed over to interrupt their money moment. "Not right now Ladies there will be time for some fun in a little bit" they smiled and walked away letting Divine know that they would be eagerly waiting for his friend. They knew the white boy had some cash and they wanted to be the first to get their hands on it. Barely fazed by the females in the room, Divine was more concerned with getting some clientele from Jeremiah; he walked Jeremiah to the back room to speak in private. "So what's up Jeremiah, you liking what you see so far? He asks as he could see the amazement in Jeremiah's face. Grinning from ear to ear Jeremiah replied. "Hell yeah, the females from my neighborhood don't have nothing on these girls right here. "Damn", shaking his head and complimenting Divine on the set up he wanted to know a little bit more about his new friend. "So D what exactly are you into. As I remember you were into selling candy when we first met looks like you selling something totally different now". Divine smiled and replied, "I most definitely am, and I have changed my money routine from that day we met on the field selling ten pieces of candy to your ass. We're making major moves". Divine had a good feeling about Jeremiah so it was very easy for him to give him a little insight. Confident he was doing the right thing by having this conversation with Jeremiah he continued. "I know you have a few friends that like to party and blow a lot of money. Get a little something to help them stay up all night." Jeremiah knew Divine was talking about cocaine and cocaine was a very popular drug at the parties he attended. Divine explained to him, that all he needed was to set up a few parties, give him a call and he would cut him in on the profits. Jeremiah made it clear money wasn't necessary but he did want a little coke for himself. "Well I'm down, as long as I can keep my father from finding out," he let Divine know his father was taking a business trip next week. "So if you guys are going to be ready by then just let me know". Divine didn't need to get ready. He already had access to large amounts of coke. He just needed more customers. Heading back to the party room, Quan and Jb caught their attention they were talking with the females that were interested in the white boy with the B.M.W. As the ladies got their flirt on "hey Mr. B.M.W, we have something we want to give you". Divine laughed and pointed in the direction of the back room. "Don't hurt him girls, he might not be able to handle all that". Jeremiah smacked one of the females on her ass and said excitingly "oh I'm going to handle it and handle it well" the two thick females escorted Jeremiah into the room, where they were planning to give him a night he would never forget. Quan wanted to know what Divine and Jeremiah were talking about in the room. He knew it had something to do with money and he wasn't intrigued at the thought of having a white boy in the crew. He looked at Divine with a smirk. "I know you're planning something and from the look on your face it's something big. I'm just trying to figure out what this white boy's being here has to do with it". It was obvious to Divine, that Quan had a problem with the white boy. If only Quan would just trust him and stop worrying so damn much things would go smoothly. Not in the mood to talk business, Divine answered Quan in a nonchalant demeanor. "I got something in the works with this dude and I need you to cut him some slack. He's not a bad person, but then again I forgot if it ain't the crew you don't fuck with anyone like that except the bitches". Quan disagreed. "Naw not all of them, some of them hoes is trifling". Divine shook his head and let his team know they were about to make some major moves. He told them about the party and mentally prepared them. Eager to get back to the party he made a gesture to his team the business part of the night was done. The party was popping, the honeys were looking right. The Get Money Crew's hood recognition grew. The party ended a little after 6 a.m. Jeremiah ended up crashing at the crib because he was too bent to drive. Divine paid one of the local dudes in the area to watch the car, no one asked questions at all, Meanwhile Jb didn't have any clue that his mother was on her way to the apartment. Quan was the first one up awakened by the knocking on the door as he walked over and looked into the peephole he saw it was an older woman knocking on the door. "Yo, Jb you got a visitor at the door" Quan called out to Jb, walking from the bedroom assuming Quan was setting him up for the door to door solicitors he said jokingly. "Nigga stop playing I'm not expecting anybody". Knowing that Jb wasn't taking him serious he looked at him with a serious look on his face. "well maybe you should because it's a woman and she look like a younger version of your grandmother'. Jb looked through the peephole in total disbelief. no way in the world did he believe his mother.(Charlene Jenkins, looking half her age, only 4 ft. tall, if you didn't know her personally you wouldn't believe she had children.) the same woman who left him with his grandmother years ago was now knocking on his door, without further hesitation Jb opens the door with a attitude. "What are you doing here?" he asked his mother as she passed him her bags. "Well hello to you too" she said as she just walked right in the house as if her name was on the lease. Looking around and displeased by what she saw she asked, "What the hell did you do to my mother's apartment, and who the hell are all these people up in here? Jb stood in the doorway staring at his mother in disgust as he listened to her bickering finally he interrupted her. "first of all they live here, something you haven't done since you were about 16 years old, and I'm not no little ass boy. So I don't know where you get off coming up in here trying to scream on anyone you better take that shit back down south with your husband". Just then, Jb's mother walked over to him gesturing her hands as if she was going to slap him in his face but he caught her just in time. **"Who in the hell do you think you're talking to Joseph Benjamin?"** she asked raising her voice. Divine and Quan looked on in shock they couldn't believe that was his name or that his mother just called him out like that. Deciding to give Jb and his mother privacy, they went back into the bedroom. Feeling embarrassed but keeping his cool Jb raised his voice right back at her. **"Straight up don't ever call me that name again, my name is Jb and don't you try to put your hands on me, it's been a long time and we need to get some shit straight. This is my place not yours and these are my friends and I really don't know why you are here and I really could care less"**. Blown that her son was talking to her in that tone Charlene replied, "you have a hell of a way of talking to your mother!" Jb looked at her as if she had just said the ultimate disrespectful thing to him. "Mother! Since when did you become my mother, the woman that I just buried was my mother. Just because you pushed me out don't make you my mother Mae Jenkins was my mother that's who raised me, that's who looked out for me and that's who I respected unlike you. Where were you when she died huh? Living it up with your new husband, see she was the only one who believed in your ass not me, I knew from the day she started getting sick that you were not coming to get me at all. Jb let go all of his built up frustrations all of his pain out that day, because all of this time he had never grieved for his grandmother, he had never spoken to his mother to let her know how much her being absent from his life hurt him. Her eyes watered as she tried to console her son. "Well I'm sorry I wasn't here Jb, I was going through some things and I should have been there for you and for my mother but I wasn't and that was my fault, I fucked up J. I'm here because I needed to get away for a while'. Jb looked at his mother assuming she wasn't telling him everything. "What's going on, where's your husband?" asked Jb as he waited to hear her answer. "My husband is back home he doesn't know I'm here, hell he probably doesn't even know I'm gone. I just need to stay here for about a week or two just to clear my head". She said as she kicked her feet up on the sofa, Jb really didn't know what to say, he knew his mother being there would put many things on hold, sure he was grown and it was his place but he didn't want his mother knowing his business. Jb walked into the room to tell Divine and Quan what was going on. Quan was the first one to ask questions. "Yo, what the fuck is up with that your mom's is out there straight wilding, what the hell is her problem. Talking like she bout to stay here, you know that shit is not going to work. Divine agreed, "Yo Jb you better think of something quick because we have a lot of shit hanging in the balance. And we can't afford to get caught up behind her being here. Jb knew they were right and he wasn't pleased with the thought of sharing his spot with his mother. "Yo, I don't know what the fuck is going on with her something just don't seem right, what made her pop up here after all these years. Let me play nice and take her out to lunch or something so I can really find out what's going on". Quan and Divine both wished him luck. Jb walked into the living room and offered to take his mother out to lunch so they could talk things over and get an understanding on things. Divine and Quan got the house in order and put things away just in case she was staying. Still thrown off by the unexpected visit from Jb's mother Quan said to Divine. "Yo I don't know about you D but something don't seem right with Jb's mom, why would she leave her so called good life to come all the way back up here to get in touch with a son she hasn't seen in eons. Talking bout she need to stay here for one to two weeks". Divine agreed, "Yeah something doesn't seem right, then she walked up in here like she owned the damn place, maybe she wants money. But how in the hell would she know we getting money like that, I doubt if she talk to anyone from around here". Divine and Quan continued to try to figure out exactly what Jb's mother really wanted. Meanwhile Jb and his mother were out at a nice restaurant; impressed by her son's taste she complimented him with a smile. "Well this is nice Jb, How many times do you bring your girlfriend here? Jb laughed at her assumptions and replied. "I've never been here and I don't have time to take any female out to eat". Shocked by her son's response she chuckled and she said. "What, you don't have time for females, a nice looking young man such as yourself don't have time for females? Jb wasn't interested in answering any more questions. He had questions of his own but it didn't look like he was going to have the chance to ask them. His mother sat across from him with more questions than a reporter did. "So what have you been up too Jb? I mean I'm not trying to get all in your business. I just want to make sure you're ok, last time I saw you, was when grandma got sick". Trying not to think about that day and the promise his mother made him, or the way he felt when he lost his grandmother. He knew he had to tell his mother something to keep her from questioning his income. "well that was a long time ago, now me and the crew we sell shirts and other nice items, hats, kicks whatever we can design". Lying his ass off but he sure wasn't going to sit across the table and tell his mother he and his friends were drug dealers. What Jb didn't know is that his mother already knew he was getting paid; she had spoken to an old friend not too long ago who had put her up on his activities. Charlene wanted to get her hands on some of the money she heard her son was making but she knew he wasn't going to give it to her. Since Jb wasn't being completely honest with her, she knew she had to get him to trust her enough to let his guard down so she could get her hands on his money. She made up a bogus ass story how her and her husband needed a break from one another and she decided to visit and make up for lost time. Jb really wasn't buying his mother's story, but he let her think she was telling a good one. After letting her know she was welcomed to stay for two weeks he excused himself from the table and stepped outside to call Divine and Quan. Once on the phone he let them know his mother would be staying for two weeks, and how they needed to play it safe because he wasn't sure if he could trust her, he advised them to put everything in a safe place. Quan reminded Jb they had to make a run to prepare for the party at Jeremiah's house; Jb told him where his re-up money was stashed at and informed them he would meet them shortly in the back of the building. Jb meets Charlene back inside the restaurant pays the bills and they head back to the apartment, he took her through the front entrance to keep her from running into Divine and Quan. Once upstairs Jb grabbed his jacket and told Charlene he had to make a few runs. Charlene kicked her feet up on the couch she didn't bother questioning her son because she had other things on her mind and one of them was to snoop through the apartment Jb headed out the door to meet up with Divine and Quan, once downstairs Divine and Quan questioned him about letting his mother stay in the apartment. Jb let them know he we keep a close eye on her and keep their street business away from his personal business. Charlene waited for a few minutes in case Jb forgot something and needed to come back once she realized he wasn't coming right back she began to snoop throughout the apartment. everyone's door was locked except for Quan's, he forgot to go back and lock it when he went to get Jb's bread out of his room, little did she know the money that she was hoping to find was gone. She entered Quan's room. "Damn he got a lot of shit in this room, expensive shit too! she thought to herself, looking around all in the closet, under the bed, behind the Dresser, just as she was about to push the Dresser back she noticed a bag taped to the back of the Dresser which turned out to be coke. Quan always kept a stash back there for the females just in case they needed an extra push to get right. Pulling the bag from the back of the dresser, she said aloud. "I know this is not what I think it is", she opened the bag up and dipped her finger in so she could taste it. "Damn" the taste of the coke enticed her. She scooped a little bit out, put everything back the way she found it closed the door, went into her bag for her make up mirror and a dollar bill and went into the bathroom so she could do her thing. Speaking aloud as she lined her coke on the mirror. "Damn I haven't sniffed coke in a while and they wasn't making it like this when I was doing it". She was so focused on getting high she didn't realize she was talking out loud to herself, she sniffed and sniffed until she found herself going back into Quan's room dipping into the stash and sniffing up all of his coke. Meanwhile Quan, Divine and Jb were almost to the pick-up location, neither one having a clue to what was going down back at the crib. Charlene had left the crib to stroll the neighborhood to find some more coke. She didn't realize that her son and his crew were the only ones in the neighborhood that dealt with that. When they got back to the crib they didn't notice anything out place, nor did Quan notice that she had been all up in his room and in his secret stash. The only thing he noticed was that he didn't lock his door, blaming Jb for his forgetfulness. "Damn I didn't even lock my door fucking with you Jb" refusing to accept Quan's blaming him, Jb replied with a smirk. "What is you talking bout you act like someone was in here, won't nobody in here but my mom's. As a matter of fact, where is my mom's? He had no idea his mother was high and on a coke hunt. Catching a chill from the a.c being on full blast Divine said "I don't know but she got the air on up in here and got a nigga freezing. I'm bout to lay down I'll catch you niggas in the a.m.". Divine headed to his room. Quan was heading to bed as well he looked over at Jb with a grin and said, "Yo I hope your mama got a key or her ass going to be outta luck". Quan headed to his room and closed the door. Jb sat up on the couch for a few hours watching a movie and just as he was about to doze off he heard the door unlocking. He jumped up and looked at his watch, shaking his head it was 4:00 in the morning, those were get money hours but due to their unexpected houseguest, the crew was on pause. Jb rolled over on the couch and went back to sleep. Charlene crept in the door and tried to be quiet as she walked to Jb's room to go lay down. The next morning everyone was up except for Charlene, Divine was on the phone with Jeremiah getting everything straight for the party they planned. Quan wasn't too comfortable Charlene being in the crib while they were out of town. He didn't need any of his jump- offs popping up running their mouth, Jb didn't like the fact that she was there but he figured her being in the house alone for the weekend wouldn't damper their hustling. Divine got the party info from Jeremiah, and was ready to roll out. Jb walked into his room and saw that Charlene was still sleeping, so he just grabbed some clothes and headed for the shower. Divine Packed all the major materials, while Quan headed out to pick up a car, # 1 rule never drive anything that could be traced back to you, so they would always get little females around the way to rent them a car for out of town trips. Charlene woke up before Divine and Jb could walk out the door, Jb pulled out a few twenty dollar bills and gave them to her letting her know they were going out of town for the weekend and would be back Sunday. Charlene gave him a hug and a kiss and grinned as she walked to the refrigerator, secretly anticipating being alone in the apartment. Jb didn't know why his mother had that look on her face, but he figured she probably was going to have a man in the crib while they were gone. He grabbed his phone off the counter and headed out the door. Charlene wasted no time to searching for more coke and money. Little did she know she wouldn't have access to anyone's room except for her Jb's and he didn't keep any drugs in there. Charlene searched in the living room, the kitchen cabinets, bathroom all through Jb's room and came up dry; her plans to get high weren't going as smooth as she thought they would. Divine, Quan and Jb finally reached the address Jeremiah gave them. Quan was impressed by the layout, he never seen a house that big in his life. "Damn Divine the white boy is living phat as hell shit I plan to be living like this real soon". Quan said as he pulled up to the driveway. Before they could put the car in park, Jeremiah met them at the car and signaled them to pull into the garage. Once inside Divine wasted no time letting Jeremiah know exactly what type of people to invite. Jeremiah called up every one he knew who loved to spend money, and who wanted to have a good time and would pay the right price to do so. Meanwhile back at the crib Charlene's search didn't turn up anything but a sneaker box filled with old pictures of her and Jb when he was younger; going through the box she noticed there was a letter addressed to Jb from an unknown sender, that hadn't been opened. She was eager to know whom the letter was from and why hadn't he opened it, but she knew if she opened it, Jb would know she had been through his things. "Oh well" Charlene thought to herself, she decided to put everything back the way she found it and call it a night. Divine and the crew were finished with their set up for the party and decided to get some rest. The next day Jeremiah took the crew to the mall to do a little shopping. "Damn do any black people shop here? Quan asked looking around noticing all the shoppers were upper-class and white. Jeremiah replied, "Only the ones with the kind of money this shopping mall requires". The four of them entered one of the men's clothing stores in the mall, as they begin to look for the right attire to wear; one of the sales associate's greeted Jeremiah. "Good morning Jeremiah". Divine, Jb and Quan looked on as Jeremiah stepped away to speak to the well-dressed female. Once he was finished with his conversation, he re-joined Divine, Jb and Quan. Wanting to know more about the sale's associate Quan asks Jeremiah if he would be inviting her to the party. Jeremiah laughs aloud and says; "hell no! Our parents have been trying to get us to hook up ever since middle school". Divine glances over and the sale associate and says, "So what's the problem? Jeremiah smiled and whispered. "The problem is she is stuck up as hell and not really my type". Disagreeing with Jeremiah, Jb says; "shit her body type look fine to me! as he glanced over in her direction.

After everyone finished trying on their clothes, they walked up to the register to pay for their purchase. The sale's associate who had spoken to Jeremiah earlier looked on as she wondered to herself who were the three black guys shopping with Jeremiah, they headed back to Jeremiah's house to get ready for the party.

****

Later on that night the party was going well. Everything was working out the way Divine had hoped it would. He didn't let anything or anyone stir him away from what his main objective was getting that money and keeping it. He would mingle with the ladies for a few minutes at a time throughout the night, but he always kept his conversations short. Never once getting caught up in the moment. Unlike Quan on the other hand his weakness was the females. Everyone in the crew knew that and warned him that the wrong one day that would be his downfall. Jb and Divine watched closely as Quan flashed his money and jewelry to the ladies by the pool. Far from impressed and trying to stay focused on the money Jb said as he continued to look on; "this nigga know we here for one reason and one reason only and he focused on some get pussy. It wasn't the first time that Quan attempted to show off in front of the ladies and it wouldn't be the last time. Divine wasn't too worried about Quan entertaining the ladies , the only thing he found odd was how Quan was against hanging with Jeremiah because he was white and now he was sitting up there trying to impress some white females. As the party continued, Divine knew he had made the right choice by deciding to keep in touch with Jeremiah after their first encounter, because it was a huge benefit to him to have a white boy as a friend especially one with money and friends with more money. Everyone Jeremiah invited was into the appetizer for the night "coke" and that was the whole purpose. The partygoers were mostly seniors in high school or freshmen in college. Most of them were introduced to coke by a friend or because they heard, stories how coke would keep them up all night. Some were either doing it because needed that boost to get them through exams or take their mind off the pressures of being perfect. Jeremiah didn't have anything to worry about as far as the party getting back to his father, who in their right mind at this kind of party would snitch. After the party was over Divine, Jb and Quan sat down to count their earnings. The stacks being laid on the table amazed Quan. "Damn we looking alright, white folks sure know how to come out they pockets." Jb looked over at Quan with a smirk and said. "how would you know nigga, your ass was too busy trying to fuck something all night" sensing Jb's animosity Quan replied, "damn Jb is you hating , shit I ain't fuck nothing, them bitches sucked me off that was it". Divine gave Quan a pound, "damn Q you on fire tonight ain't you? Divine said as he and Jb busted out in laughter. Divine continued on,

"Naw fo'real it's all good nigga you do what you do. you love the ladies you can't change that, we came here to get this money and we got it" before Divine could finish his sentence Jeremiah cut in and said "there's plenty more where that came from, my damn phone won't stop ringing , damn near everyone that was here is trying to get some more of that powder". Divine was pleased as he responded to Jeremiah. "That's cool but we not going to keep doing the party thing that was just a little introduction, we'll work something out as far as clientele goes. Besides, we wouldn't want your neighbors to start to getting suspicious. Every time your pops goes out of town, calling up them blue boys". Jeremiah agreed and suggested they tried a different approach, the night was over everyone was drained from the party they crashed in the living room. The next morning Divine, Jb and Quan packed up everything and headed back to the hood, Jeremiah called up a cleaning service to clean up the house and get everything in order before his father returned. Once back in the hood Jb and Quan headed back to the crib while Divine went to pay a visit to Ace, whom he kept distant from the crew for his own reasons. It was always good to keep certain people in the cut. Divine would visit Ace for advice, even though Ace always told him if he ever came across a problem to let him know and he would help him out. Luckily, everything was going smooth for Divine; he hadn't crossed that bridge yet. Ace was always happy to see Divine; because he respected the man, he had become a true moneymaker, he also like the fact that Divine was strong minded, respectful and on point with everything. The two of them sat down and conversed. As always, Ace had a story to tell. "Hey D, I just sent my girls out to the mall to go get some nice items for this trip we're taking this weekend, you know I have to stay on top of this pimping shit. I don't miss a beat and them bitches don't miss a dollar you hear me". Ace joked as he poured himself a drink, he grabbed a extra glass and offered Divine a drink, Divine declined with a smile and said "you know I don't drink or smoke, a clear head gets bread a clogged one gets a bullet" Ace agreed with Divine on that note. They sat around catching up on things. Meanwhile back at the crib Quan and Jb walked in on Charlene entertaining herself, blasting some old jams and singing right along. Charlene noticed Jb and Quan walking in the door and turned the radio down to greet them. "Hey y'all back already, Jb I was going through your grandmother's old records, I didn't think she kept these, the way she used to get on me about listening to them". Jb noticed Charlene had cleaned up while they were gone, feeling relieved that nothing was out of place, he thought to himself, "so far so good". As they were talking, Quan walked in his room to put his bags away and tuck away some powder he had left over from the party. when he pulled the Dresser back he noticed the last bit of stash was missing, at first he didn't think nothing of it he just assumed he had used it up the night of the last party in the crib. He was so bent that night he really couldn't remember,

He tucked the stash, and headed to the shower. Charlene knew that Jb and his friends went out of town to either pick up or distribute. She was waiting for them to slip up so she could get lucky. Jb still didn't know his mother's reasons for being there and the more he asked the more she gave him her lame ass excuse for just needing some time away. He didn't want to stress himself over it, he was just ready for her to leave and according to his calendar it would be soon. Charlene still wanted to dip her hands in the money she had heard her son was sitting on but her mind was starting to stray, getting high wasn't part of her plan but it had become part of her desire. Divine had got back to the crib and was ready to do some heavy planning. He decided on the drive back that the crew needed to get up on something else; they never stayed with the same drug for long. Divine always took any ideas he had to Jb first. He was always focused on getting money and always ready for a change, they knew Quan would be down regardless. Before they began conversing Charlene grabbed her jacket and told Jb she was going out for a while, little did he know she was going on a coke hunt. She needed to get high and she knew they wouldn't be leaving out anytime soon to give her time to snoop. Charlene headed out, while Divine and Jb sat down at the table. Divine told Jb he wanted to start fucking with heroin, sure the coke game was looking good but the dope game was looking even better. Crack money was good too. But some local niggas were already fucking with that. As Quan was exiting, the bathroom he overheard Jb and Divine talking, they told him the plan and put him in charge of the coke part of the game, Quan didn't have any complaints the money was good and the bitches he would hit off would do some things on it. The rules of the game were to stay a step ahead of everyone else and that's just what the G.M.C set out to do. They had made it this far without getting caught up and they weren't planning on stopping for anything or anyone. Charlene was back from her search it was another dry night, noticing everyone was still up she asked them if they wanted to play spades. They agreed and Charlene pulled out a deck of cards her and Jb teamed up against Quan and Divine. Charlene shuffled the cards as Quan, Jb and Divine sat at the table prepared to kill some time. Throughout the game Quan kept reneging, he had never really played spades before; he never had the time he was always running errands for his mother or babysitting. Jb and Charlene were racking up on the books they knew exactly what cards to play and how to come out with a winning hand, finally after going into the hole for the third time Quan decided to quit and call it a night. "Shit I'm tired I'm going to lay down". Jb laughed and replied. "You need to nigga cause you ain't playing cards" Divine was tired as well, so he threw his hand in and went to bed. Charlene enjoyed the game and went to bed as well. The next morning, Divine, Quan and Jb followed their normal routines, handling transactions as usual. Jeremiah called to let Divine know that the coke was in high demand, so he needed to get up there quick, Divine was happy to hear that them white folks was loving the product, he knew that the crew would never go broke, cause white money never came up funny, and he was all about getting every way possible.

The beginning of the end Chapter 4

Divine walked into Quan's room to let him know what he and Jeremiah needed some powder. "Yo! Q, you gotta make a run up to meet J, and make sure you have enough cause he said it's crucial up there, Jb and I are going to go handle that thing we talked about, so I guess we'll meet up later". Quan grabbed his keys. Eager to take a ride up to whiteyville he said with a grin, "Aight cool I got that I'm going to roll out right now" Quan left to go meet up with Jeremiah, while Jb and Divine headed to go meet some connects. Charlene didn't even notice they were gone, as she came out the room she looked around and realized she was the only one in the house, she tried to open Divine's door. "Damn this nigga always lock his door he must have a gold mind up in here or something" She thought to her self as she tried to turn the knob to enter Divine's room. She tried Quan's door and just her luck it was unlocked "good he forgot to lock it". She was anxious as she entered his room, not looking for money but looking right behind the Dresser where she found the last bag of coke. "bingo" her eyes lit up as she ripped the bag off of the back of the Dresser without any hesitation and begin to get high she was so caught up in the moment that she didn't even leave the room. She sat right on the floor with her mirror and her dollar bills and sniffed damn near everything in the bag. Meanwhile Divine and Jb were still driving they had a long way before they got to their destination but Quan was on his way back to the crib. He had went and handled his biz and was done, them fiends in Whiteville wiped him out. Charlene was so into her high that she didn't even here Quan entering into the apartment, as Quan walked in he noticed Jb, Divine hadn't made it back yet, and he noticed that his room door was wide open. "Damn I didn't even lock my door," he thought to himself as he walked into his room. First thing, he noticed was his Dresser pulled away from the wall and Charlene was sitting on the floor with her back turn away from him. "What the fuck are you doing?" Quan yelled as he realized Charlene had been in his coke. She looked up at him but she was too high to realize that she had fucked up by being in his room. "You a fucking fiend, you all up in here sniffing shit like you paid for it" Quan said with a look of disgust on his face as Charlene got up from the floor and wiped the powder residue from her nose. "first of all who you talking to like that I am Jb's mother and you need to show me some respect" Charlene said as she attempted to put her hands in Quan's face but he wasn't trying to hear what the hell her high ass had to say. "Bitch is you crazy? Respect is the last thing you getting from me, you up in my shit, touching shit that doesn't belong to you and you talking about respect. Shit you ain't nothing but a little fiend as bitch to me right about now and you owe me for that shit you done soaked up your fucking nose". Quan stood in front of Charlene as if he was going to hit her any respect he had for her was officially gone. "What you want some money?" I didn't even take that much of your shit. Charlene said as she grabbed the bag and slammed it on the dresser. She was lying but she didn't care. As she tried to walk out of the room, Quan blocked the door; her petite frame was no match for him at 6 ft. tall. "I don't want your money I got something else in mind," Quan said in a grimy tone as he grabbed her by her belt buckle. "You need to get out of my way before I tell my son you were up in here starting shit with me".

Charlene said as she realized that she was in a fucked up situation. "Oh you going to tell your son, that nigga don't give a fuck about you and once he find out you a fucking coke fiend he really ain't going to give a fuck". Said Quan as he pushed her onto the bed, yanking her pants off and began forcing himself into her. Charlene pleaded with him to stop as he continued to violate her repeatedly. When he was finished, he pulled his penis out, forced in her mouth, and made her perform oral sex on him. Quan moaned as he ejaculated inside of her mouth then he pushed Charlene to the side and got up from the bed. Charlene lay stiffened with pain from what she had just encountered by then her high was gone and she was in a state of shock and disbelief. "Get the fuck up and get the fuck out" Quan said as he signaled Charlene out of his room. "And if you tell anyone about what happened up in here I'm going to kill you". Charlene grabbed her ripped clothes as she listened to Quan's threats she went into the bathroom to clean herself up. Quan knew he had to clean up the room, there was blood on the sheets, so he grabbed everything threw it into a laundry bag lit some incense and headed to the Laundromat. Charlene came out of the bathroom and noticed that Quan was gone, she knew she had to get out of there fast before he came back knowing she wouldn't be able to look her son in the face while telling him what had happened. She grabbed her belongings and decided to write Jb a note before she left. "Dear Jb, I decided to cut my stay short, I talked to my husband and we worked everything out, so I'm heading home, thank you for letting me stay, take care of yourself love always, Charlene". She left the apartment but she wasn't going back home to her husband, she got herself a room at a hotel not too far from the apartment. Jb and Divine were on their way back to the crib when they noticed Quan leaving from the Laundromat; Divine beeped the horn at Quan as they proceeded to follow him back to the apartment. "damn that nigga doing laundry early" Jb said as he and Divine just assumed that he was getting ready to have some company over, since that's the only time he did laundry. As they headed into the apartment, Jb wondered where his mother was. "I guess she making her rounds at the store" Jb said as he unlocked his door when he entered his room he found the note that Charlene left on the bed. "Yo, she left yo, my mom's went back down south to her husband, damn she could have waited til I got back" Jb said upsettingly as he showed Divine the note his mother left for him. Quan looked at Jb with a blank look on his face, knowing he was the reason for her leaving, but he wasn't going to let Jb or Divine know what had happened, deep down he was happy to know that Charlene had left and didn't tell Jb what had happened. "Damn your mom's just broke out huh?" Divine said as he walked over to the couch where Quan was sitting "What's up Quan how did everything turn out with J?" Divine asked as he wondered if Quan made it to and from Whiteyville. "Everything went smooth, I put the bread up in the closet it was a clean sweep up there," Quan said as he assured Divine it was a good night. Divine looked at Quan with a smirk and said "I see your ass getting ready to bang something up in the room you doing laundry and shit". Quan shook his head with a uninterested look on his face "I'm not up for no bitches tonight I'm just going to fall back". Divine thought it was strange for Quan to be doing Laundry in the middle of the week and not be expecting company. Jb looked over at Quan in shock "Damn Q either you tired as hell or you jumped off with one of them broads when you went to go meet up with J". Quan stood up grabbed his phone and walked towards his bedroom door. "Naw I ain't jump off I'm just tired."Quan went into his room and began to make the bed; images of what he had done to Charlene kept flooding through his mind. Divine and Jb sat up putting together the work they picked up so they could get it out to the block, they knew they had to do it up right because one fuck up would put a stop in their flow . "Yo D we bout to crush them with this shit here" said Jb as he got everything in order, by the end of the night they were ready to hit the block. Quan stayed to himself the whole night, wondering if Charlene would ever come back and tell her son what he had did to her. He knew if that day ever came that he would have deal with it quick. Jb and Divine followed their normal routine, the money was coming in fast and in large amounts, the fiends had no complaints at all. The get money crew was on their way to the top. Meanwhile back in Whiteyville Jeremiah's father was really riding his back about going to law school. Jeremiah felt overpowered by his father's plans for his future he didn't want to be a lawyer but he knew he couldn't let his father down, Divine hadn't spoken to Jeremiah in a few days, so he had no idea that Jeremiah was on his way to law school. Quan was trying to get Divine and Jb to make some moves to find another spot to lay their heads. "Yo Jb we need to get up outta here soon cause we getting too large to be around this bitch like this sooner or later niggas is going to get in their heads that they can have what we have and niggas is going to try to be on some snake shit". Quan said as he tried to convince Jb and Divine to go along with his plans to move out of the hood. "Niggas know who we are and how we get down ain't nobody going to try to cross that line and end up bodied" Divine said and he lifted up his shirt showing off his piece. He wasn't down for the move, he loved being in the hood and he wasn't afraid of anything or anyone. "Damn Q let me find out you feeling like a bitch what's with all the move talk?" Jb said as he noticed the look on Quan's face was serious. He didn't know why Quan wanted to get out of the hood so bad but he wasn't buying the story that Quan was trying to sell. Quan looked at Jb with a tight grill "nigga I ain't no bitch, I just think we need to go a step further and get the fuck up from round here, what y'all nigga going to live in this crib for the rest of y'all lives". Quan had his true reasons for wanting to move. He didn't want to be anywhere close by if Charlene decided to pop back up. "But damn Quan you acting like it's a problem with being here, you know something we don't know? What the fuck has you shook that you want to get out of the hood, shit money is looking good right now but not that fucking good we doing our thing we not hot with them blue boys so shit is ok. We're gonna do big things real soon but not right now, think about it we move to a new spot where niggas don't know us and start watching us then it's going to be a problem and then what do you think is going to happen?" Divine said as he tried to keep his team in the hood but Quan was still determined to move on. "I'm just saying I want more than this! Quan continued with his move out of the hood suggestions. Divine and Jb didn't know what was really going on with Quan; he was always the loudest one in the crew, the one who was always quick to react if there was a problem and now he was sitting across from them acting like a completely different person. Across town in a hotel room Charlene found herself plotting revenge against Quan for what he had done to her. Yeah he had every right to be upset with her for sniffing up his shit but to rape her than threaten to take her life that was fucked up. She wasn't exactly going to go back to the apartment and tell Jb what his so-called boy did to her. She had her mind set on exactly how she was going to get his ass back. In her spare time if she wasn't plotting on Quan she was getting high her addiction grew and she couldn't stay away from it. She needed to support her habit so she bought a blonde wig and a few outfits from a local exotic store to hit the streets. Just as she was coming out of the store, she noticed a car pulling up alongside her with tinted windows. "damn who the fuck is this" she thought to herself hoping it wasn't anyone trying to start some shit with her as she looked over to the car the windows rolled down and she couldn't believe it was Quan "what the fuck?" she thought as she stared at the nigga who threatened to take her life. She was shocked she hadn't expected to see him any time soon. "Get in the car" Quan said angrily as he opened the door. As bad as Charlene wanted to run she knew she couldn't out run a car, so she got in. "what the fuck are you doing around here ain't you supposed to be gone?" Quan asked as he began to drive. Charlene rolled her eyes and said " I wasn't ready to leave, why the fuck are you worried about what I'm doing any way I'm not bothering you and I'm not going to tell my son what you did to me". Quan wasn't moved by Charlene attitude and he smirk and said" I know you're not going to tell your son anything cause you wanna live right, so you need to care your ass back down south". Charlene's refusal to leave town angered

Quan. He threatened to take her directly to the bus station. Charlene could tell by the look on his face he was serious so she agreed to leave town but not until she picked up her things from her hotel room. Charlene didn't want Quan to know what room she was in and tried to talk him into letting her out a few blocks away, Quan didn't trust her to go and come right back so he ordered her to show him where her hotel was at. Charlene directed Quan to the hotel as they entered the room he pulled some coke out of his jacket pocket, Charlene wanted to get high so bad but she wasn't sure why he was trying to give it to her so freely. "You know you want some," Quan said as he teased her with the bag. He waved it back and forth in front of her. Charlene tried her best to turn the offer down. " I don't mess with that any more so put it away" Quan wasn't buying it in his eyes once a fiend always a fiend he walked closer to her and said, "stop playing you know you want some", Charlene tried to change the subject and focus on packing her stuff and leaving the room. Quan wasn't in a rush to leave the room he had Charlene right where he wanted her he sat the coke down on the table and went into the bathroom. While he was in the bathroom, he took off all of his clothes and waited a few minutes for Charlene to give in and get her sniff on. Charlene tried to stay away from the bag but she couldn't she dumped all the powder on the table and begin sniffing like crazy, just then Quan came out of the bathroom, noticing Charlene fell right into his trap he mumbled. "I knew you couldn't leave that shit alone" Charlene looked up as Quan walked towards her, she was so into the powder she didn't even notice that he had a hard on. Quan stood in front of her with a sick grin on his face while rubbing on his manhood. He pulled her over to the bed she didn't even try to fight Quan. She just laid there; blanked out as he raped her repeatedly. Quan could have any female he wanted but what he was doing to Charlene had nothing to do with attraction. It was all about control and he loved having that power. Once he was finished he put on his clothes and directed Charlene to grab her things. He drove her to the bus station bought her a one-way ticket and waited for her bus to arrive. Charlene boarded the bus station thinking to herself how was she going to get out of this, she knew Quan wasn't going to leave until she bus pulled off. She handed the bus driver her ticket and took her seat. Quan stood there until the bus pulled off. "I'm coming back mother fucker" Charlene thought to herself as the bus pulled off, Quan got back in his car and went back to the house, when he got in Jb and Divine weren't there, so Quan got in the shower and called up some females for the night. Divine and Jb had went to the club just to chill out for a while. They didn't bother calling Quan since he was acting like he was on some solo shit. They decided to give him some space. At the club, Jb was trying to enjoy the atmosphere but he was feeling some kind of way about Quan's being distant. He looked over at Divine and said "Yo D what the fuck is up with Quan that nigga is on some other shit right now". Divine noticed as well that Quan was acting a little different but he was quite sure as to why. He knew eventually everything would come to light. Meanwhile on the bus Charlene was waiting for her chance to get off. The driver announced that he would be stopping in a few minutes; Charlene grabbed her purse and waited for the bus to stop once off the bus she went inside the rest area to grab something to eat. Fifteen minutes had past and she heard the bus driver calling out for the passengers to return to the bus. She wasn't getting back on the bus headed down south. She was going back to New York. Charlene walked up to the ticket counter to purchase a one way to New York. She was going back to make sure Quan did not get away with what he did to her. She also felt if he would violate her knowing she is his best friend's mother, eventually he would turn on her son. Her ulterior motive had changed she didn't want the money; she didn't want the drugs she wanted to protect Jb and deal with Quan. The bus for New York pulled into the station and Charlene was on her way back to NY. Jb and Divine headed back to the apartment. As they walked in, they could hear that Quan had company. The music was on and his door was closed. Drained from a long as day they called it a night. The next day Divine got up and began to make some phone calls, he thought he would call up Jeremiah and see what was going on with him. Every time he would call the number he had for Jeremiah the phone would just ring. Divine had no idea that Jeremiah was no longer into the party life. He gave it all up and listened to his father. Jeremiah was attending law school. Divine hung the phone up after trying two more times, just then Quan came out of the room and spoke to Divine "what's good D? Laughing at the fact that Quan was in a good mood Divine replied, "I guess you are nigga after all that noise that was coming from your room last night" With a smirk Quan replied, "shit you know them birds don't know how to act, what's up with Jb? Divine replied, "he's still sleep I tried to call J on the phone but I'm not getting an answer, I know if something was wrong we would have heard something" Quan seemed concern and volunteered to drive up to check on Jeremiah but Divine said he would just wait to hear from him. Quan told Divine that he was headed to Philly for the weekend to handle some business with his cousin Raymond. Divine didn't have a problem with Quan going out of town, every member in the crew had things that they handled solo. Quan was out the door and headed to Philly. Jb was awakened by his cell phone ringing. He reached over to answer it, the voice on the other end whispered "watch the company you keep." then hung up Jb tried to check his phone's caller I'd for the number but it was a blocked number. Not knowing what the call was about he got up and went into the kitchen and told Divine what had just happened. "Yo I just got some weird ass call to my phone something about watch the company I keep" Divine looked over at Jb and could tell he wasn't joking but neither one of them had a clue who was playing on his cellphone. Just then, the house phone began to ring. Divine picked up the phone. The voice on the other end whispered to him "watch the company you keep" and hung up" Divine hung up the phone, and said to Jb as he shook his head, "what the fuck now they calling the crib" Jb and Divine did not know what was going on or why someone was calling and whispering on the phone. they sat around waiting to see if the person would call back. Quan was finally in Philly; he met up with his cousin Raymond and was ready to handle his business. Raymond wasn't deep in the hustle game like Quan, Jb or Divine. Even though he sold weed in large quantities, his love was robbing niggas who had a little bit more than he had. Raymond had his eyes set on some niggas he heard was getting major paper and he wanted Quan to ride with him to hit them up. Quan didn't give a fuck and Raymond knew he would have his back if some shit went down. Raymond handed Quan a .380 and a ski mask and headed out the door, to go meet up with the rest of his team. The dudes than Raymond ran with were stick up kids always looking for a bag to snatch or a nigga to rob when Raymond put them on to the big money they were more than willing to be down. Raymond found a local nigga who needed a few dollars and paid him to be their driver. Once plans were made everyone was in the car, Raymond directed the driver to the spot where everything was about to go down and began to give out the rules of robbery. "look this ain't no game right here, we going to go in there, do what we gotta do and bounce if a nigga wanna jump best believe we going to pop some hot ones in his ass" Raymond said as he loaded up his piece. Everyone was strapped and ready to go. Quan looked over at his cousin and the stick up kids in the car put his mask on and said. "let's do this" they creeped out the car and ran up in the crib guns drawn, the niggas they were robbing were some new jack hustlers who seemed to think they ass wouldn't get jacked, they thought wrong Raymond and the crew took everything jewelry, money, anything of value and made them niggas strip down to their boxers. "Nobody move nobody get blasted up in this bitch!" Raymond said as he backed out of the apartment door, running to the car. Once inside the car he ordered the driver to get the fuck from around there. They sped off and headed back to the crib to lay low. Quan was hype he had never robbed anyone before it gave him a rush, lifting up the bags of goods he said to his cousin. "Damn that shit was easier than taking candy from a baby! agreeing with his cousin Raymond replied, those niggas ain't nobody, they moved around here like a year ago call they selves hustling and shit, them niggas is pussy and stupid as hell" Quan sat back and looked at his cousin and said, "damn that couldn't of been me and my niggas. I would have put a hole in a nigga up soon as he came in the door talking some robbery shit." The stick up kids stared at Quan as Raymond responded. "Those niggas weren't expecting any shit like that to happen to them. That's supposed to be a low- low crib. Some bitches I know gave me the 411 on them niggas a while ago, shit leave it to a bitch to run her damn mouth". Everyone is the car agreed on that one. They finally pulled up to the crib, Raymond told the driver to get rid of the car while they went to chill, smoke a blunt and talk about their night. Raymond wanted to know how Quan and his team were making out; it had been a while since they copped any weed from him. "Yo Q what's going on with your team down there? Quan took a pull of the blunt and asked with a smirk, "What nigga you going to rob me too? Raymond laughed as he replied "Naw nigga you family, I'm just saying you the type of nigga who doesn't have to do this but you did and I respect you for riding with me" Quan was loyal to his fam, above anyone else. Quan let Raymond know that he and his team were crushing the drug game. Jb and Divine handled the brown sugar and he handles the chyna white. Shocked to hear his cousin was only handling the chyna white Raymond asked Quan "whose idea was that? Quan replied. "Those niggas decided but I'm not tripping either way all of the money is getting split three ways" not understanding how his cousin could be content with the fat that Divine and Jb were teaming up on a product and put him on a product solo Raymond continued on with his views. "So let me get this straight these to niggas make the rules and you follow them. Those niggas is fucking with the big bank messing with that brown sugar. Don't get me wrong, that white is a good money maker to but damn" Quan was listening but honestly it didn't bother him he didn't mind slanging the coke, a lot of bitches he dealt with used coke so it gave him a boost with the ladies. Quan made it clear he would fuck a bitch high off of the coke any day over a bitch high off the horse. Raymond and Quan sat around smoking and talking about bitches, money and life. Quan was so high he ended up letting it slip on what had happened with Jb's mother Charlene. "Yo cuz let me tell you some bugged out shit," he said as he passed Raymond the blunt. Raymond was high but he was still coherent as to what was being said to him he sat there as Quan continued. "That nigga Jb mom's was staying with us. She popped up one day acting like she was running shit at first. Then she calmed down, well come to find out this bitch was a fiend. I had left my door unlocked one day trying to rush and handle my b.i came back this bitch was in my room sniffing up my little stash I had tucked away, yo I fucked that bitch up, fucked her in every hole too." Raymond put the blunt down, and looked over at Quan and said, "Say word nigga! Quan didn't have any shame with him as he bragged on. "That's my word nigga" Raymond still stunned by hat his cousin had just told him shook his head and asked, "do Jb know that shit went down? Quan told him Jb didn't know what happened and proceeded to tell his cousin the rest of the story. "I made that bitch bounce from the crib and she was supposed to take her ass back home. I'm on the strip one day and I see this bitch coming out the hair store snatched her up got her ass again put her ass on the next thing smoking back down south". Raymond warned Quan to watch himself because if word got back to Jb it was going to be a problem. Quan let him know that if that day ever came he would kill a nigga before a nigga killed him. Raymond looked at his cousin shocked to hear him talking about how he would kill his right hand man. He also knew the rules of the streets; kill a nigga first before he kills you. He knew that Quan was dead ass serious by what he was saying. Quan was feeling his drink and the blunt. He told Raymond how he wanted to move out of the crib but Divine and Jb weren't feeling the idea as if they were scared to move and shit. Raymond asked Quan if he wanted to move to Philly with him. Quan laughed and replied, "Hell no nigga so you can stick me up" imitating his cousin Raymond. "This is a mother fucking robbery!" Raymond starts laughing and says, "Well nigga do your thing, if them niggas don't want to make moves then you make it for them. Only one nigga can wear the crown. " Raymond knew exactly what he was saying to Quan, he knew if Quan got on some solo shit and stopped fucking with Jb and Divine there would be room for him to pull in that paper. Quan dapped his cousin up and replied. "You damn right I'm going to make moves with or without them niggas." Quan ended up passing out on the couch, Raymond threw a blanket over him and went to bed. The next morning Quan was awake but didn't remember half of what he said last night. Little did he know Raymond did word for word. "Good morning king Q," Raymond said as walked to the kitchen. Quan had a hangover and was starving he looked around the kitchen and asked "what's for breakfast, where the pancakes and sausage at? Raymond laughed as he replied. "The only sausage that gets served in here is for the bitches and we're the only ones here" Quan Bust out laughing and decided to go out for breakfast. They headed to a local diner and ordered a banging breakfast. After breakfast, Quan headed back to New York.

Money is the root of all evil Chapter 5

The get money crew was on top of their game getting money and keeping it. But in every crew there was always one person who wanted it all and the person was Quan. He was starting to feel some kind of way and he no longer wanted to be part of the team. Divine and Jb didn't even see it coming, Quan became more and more distant from the crew. He was spending most of his time in Philly with his cousin or with some honeys in a telly.

****

Divine decided to take a drive to Whiteyville to see what was up with Jeremiah and why he hadn't heard from him. As he arrived, a well-dressed woman greeted him. He wasn't sure if this was Jeremiah's mother, the woman had informed him that Jeremiah had moved and he was in law school and that he really didn't visit much. Divine couldn't believe was he was hearing. "Damn" he thought to himself as he got in his car and drove off. He was trying to figure everything out, Jeremiah never mentioned anything to him about law school, and he didn't even call him to let him know that he was going. On his way back to the hood Divine got a call from Jb stating he was going to meet someone and that he would meet up with him later, Divine decided to handle some business before went back to the crib. Earlier in the day, Jb had received a phone call and the caller gave him an address. Jb wasn't nervous to go alone he took his heat with him just in case it was some crazy shit about to go down. Jb pulled up to the address and got out of the car. as he was walking up to the building he noticed a woman sitting on the steps with

71

her head down. To his surprise, it was his mother. Charlene didn't really know where to begin she just stood up and hugged her son tighter than she ever hugged him before. Jb wasn't sure why she wanted to meet with him away from the house but he was ready to hear her out. She took him inside the building and begins to explain. " first of all I need you to know that I love you with all my heart, no matter how you may see things I do love you, when I wrote you that letter I said that I had went back home. Well I didn't, I couldn't, I was still up here trying to figure some things out. I couldn't stay in that apartment with you and your friends" Charlene wanted to tell him so bad what had happened with Quan but she wasn't sure how he would react. She wanted to get even with Quan for what he had did to her but she didn't want Jb to be in the middle of it. Jb could tell something was bothering Charlene but he figured she would tell him when the time was right. He decided to take her out to eat to get her mind off whatever was bothering her. While they were waiting for their food, Jb got a call from Divine. "What up D?,Jb asked as he answered his phone. Divine was calling to check on him and make sure he wasn't caught up in no bullshit. He told Jb how he drove up to Whiteyville and a woman told him Jeremiah was in law school. Jb couldn't believe what he was hearing. "Damn that's crazy right there I'm sitting here with my mom's getting our eat on". Shocked to hear Charlene was back in town Divine replied, "word, when she get back up here? Jb told Divine he would fill him in later and that he was on his way to drop her off at a hotel. Divine headed back to the crib once he got in he noticed Quan was sitting on the couch counting some money. Divine looked over at Quan and said, "What up stranger I see you getting that money together" Quan looked up with a smirk and replied. "This is my cut right here I already put the rest of the money up." Divine didn't bother to check the safe and before the thought could cross his mind, Quan asked about Jb. Divine told Quan that Jb was with Charlene and would be in after he dropped her off at her hotel room. After hearing that Quan got real quiet he knew if Charlene was with Jb there was a good chance she was going to tell him what had happened and he knew that when he got to the house some shit was going to pop off. Quan didn't know if he should wait around for Jb to get back in the crib or break out and break out for good. Charlene and Jb were finished eating and Charlene wanted to go back to her room, Jb couldn't understand why his mother was determined to stay at a hotel. On the way to the hotel Jb asked Charlene, "you sure you don't want to come to the crib? She didn't want to go anywhere near that apartment because she knew Quan would be there. She held in her tears as she replied. "I'll be fine, I won't be here too long I just wanted to see you and make sure you were ok, I'll be leaving out tomorrow night" Jb had no clue that his mother was plotting her revenge against Quan. As they pulled up to the hotel, he gave Charlene some money and told her to call him if she needed anything. Charlene hugged her son and whispered in his ear; "I love you". Jb headed back to the crib, unsure why Charlene refused to come with him back to the crib she was acting real strange and Jb couldn't figure out why. As he got in Divine was in the living room and Quan was in his room. Divine wanted to know why Charlene didn't want to come to the crib. Jb told him how she was acting very strange but she wouldn't exactly tell him what was bothering her. Quan sat in his room listening to the whole conversation. He even heard Jb tell Divine that she was on a hotel by 41st Street. He could tell by Jb's tone that Charlene didn't tell him what had happened. He knew that he had to find her and deal with her quick. The next morning while Divine and Jb were asleep Quan headed out to see if he could find Charlene. He remembered Jb saying she was in a hotel by 41st street he pulled up to the block and decided to chill until he saw her. A few hours had past and Quan finally saw Charlene walking towards the hotel. He hopped out of the car and ran up to her; "I see that you can't follow simple directions" Charlene looked at him without even blinking as she replied, "I needed to come back because I have some unfinished business to take care of." Quan grabbed her by her arm and asked, "What unfinished business could you possibly have? Charlene knew that if she didn't handle Quan soon or he would only keep taunting her. She wanted to get his ass back in the worst way. She invited him inside her hotel room. Little did Quan know Charlene had written a letter to Jb and hid it in her room just in case something was to happen to her. Quan followed Charlene into the hotel room as soon as the door was closed he tried to choke her. "didn't I tell your ass to get the fuck outta here, why the fuck is you playing with me? Quan's eyes were bloodshot red as he tried to squeeze the life of her. Charlene begged him to let her go but he just squeezed tighter, Charlene was able to reach into her jacket pocket and grab her box cutter, she pulled it out and slashed Quan on his arm. "ahhh you bitch! Quan yelled as he backed up. Charlene decided this was her chance to get his ass. She slung a chair at Quan causing him to stumble towards the bed; Charlene charged him and starting slicing him up. Quan tussled with her to get the box cutter.

After a few punches to her face he was able to get it out of her hand. "Bitch what the fuck is wrong with you, you got me bleeding and shit. Oh you bout to get fucked up for this! Quan said as he slung her on the floor and began to stomp her. Grabbing her punching her all in her face Charlene was knocked unconscious, Quan picked her up and put her on the bed and raped her one last time. When he was finished, he went into the bathroom to clean himself up. As he was coming out, he heard Charlene begging him to leave her alone; he grabbed his gun, pointed to her head, and told her to put on some clothes. Once Charlene was dressed, Quan made her leave the hotel room with him. While in the car, Charlene continued to question Quan about where he was taking her. She noticed they weren't going in the direction of the bus station. It didn't look like the direction to the bus station. Charlene began to threaten Quan; "my son is going to fucking kill you nigga, you think he don't know what you did he knows everything" Quan knew she was bluffing and he wasn't worried about Jb at all. After hours of driving he finally reached a closed off road that led to a ravine located near upstate New York. Quan made her get out of the car he looked at Charlene with the coldest look and asked her the last question she would ever be asked; "you ready to die bitch? Quan pulled out his gun and shot Charlene four times. He picked her body up and threw it into the ravine. He knew he had to cover up his tracks so he made a quick call to Divine and told him a bogus ass story about him being at the clinic with one of his birds getting the A-1 special. Divine wasn't surprised because Quan always bragged how he had unprotected sex with every female he slept around with. Once he finished talking to Divine, He headed back to the freeway.

He knew he had to clean the car up, stop at the pharmacy, and get some peroxide and gauze pads to patch up. Divine and Jb were handling business as usual Jb was planning to stop by the hotel to check on his mom after he finished. "What up with that nigga Q? Jb asked as Divine hung up the phone with Quan. "That nigga at the clinic with some young ass bird getting that A-1 special" replied Divine. They both knew it wasn't the first time Quan had to pay for an abortion, they also weren't that crazy to run up in anything raw. Divine and Jb finished putting in their daily work and Jb decided he would go check on Charlene tomorrow.

****

Meanwhile, Quan had cleaned his car. He found some sweats and a white shirt in his trunk and changed his clothes. He stopped at the pharmacy and got what he needed to patch up and decided to go check out one of his broads for the night instead of going to the crib. He knew he had to get right mentally before he walked up in the crib, never once regretting what he had done. In his mind he wasn't wrong at all he also knew sooner or later he had to get at Jb before his actions came back to haunt him. The next day Jb drove by the hotel to check on Charlene. He knocked and knocked on the door but she didn't answer he called the room but she didn't answer. "Damn where the fuck is she? He thought to himself. He decided to leave a note on the door telling her to call him. He figured she was out shopping since that was what she loved to do. Jb headed back in the crib, Divine was already fixing up the food for the block, shocked to see Jb back so soon "damn you back already? Divine asked as Jb walked in the door. My mom's, wasn't even there, I guess she out shopping as usual", Divine was ready for the work to hit the block. "Call that nigga Q and see where he at so he can go dish this shit out if not I'll go do it" Divine said as he bagged up the product. "Damn that nigga ain't come through yet! Let me find out he laid up with shorty after he done took her to the clinic." said Jb as he called Quan's phone he didn't get a answer so he just left a message. "Yo that nigga ain't picking up". Quan was finally on his way in the crib he knew that Divine and Jb would have plenty of questions so he was prepared. He never checked his voicemail; he was too busy trying to cover what he had done. Jb heard Quan as he was walking in the door. "Damn nigga I was blowing your phone up why you ain't hit me back? Quan tried to play it cool as he responded to Jb. "My bad, I was wrapped up in something" Divine looked over and said. "I hope not in no pussy" Jb and Divine, joked on about Quan keeping the abortion clinics in business. "Y'all niggas crazy, I was running around picking up a few things I dropped shorty off and broke out." Jb shook his head as he replied "yeah I heard nigga, we told your ass stop feeding them bitches raw meat" Quan grabbed his crotch and said "stop for what y'all know raw dick keep em thick." Divine passed the work to Quan and asked if he was going to hit the block but Quan decided to stay in the crib claiming he was tired from ripping and running all day. Divine and Jb headed for the block, Quan sat in the crib was playing everything back in his head. He knew there was no turning back from what he had done. The fact that he has just murdered his right hand man mom's didn't really bother him.

Jb and Divine were finished putting the work out on the block and Jb was starting to get a little worried because Charlene hadn't called him yet. He decided to drive back over to the hotel, this time Divine decided to ride with him. As Jb pulled up he could see the note was still on the door, he walked around the hotel asking a few people had they seen her or heard her in her room. Everyone gave him the same response, They saw Charlene come and go as usual. The housekeeper overheard Jb asking about Charlene she walked over and told him that she had seen a young man with a nice car come by the hotel and how Charlene didn't look happy to see him. She also mentioned that when she saw Charlene leaving the room she had her head down and her and the young man left. Something didn't seem right to Jb as he listened to the housekeeper describe Charlene's demeanor he asked the housekeeper was the young man that she saw black on white. The housekeeper told him the young man was black and had a very nice car. Jb wanted her to open up the room but she wasn't allowed to go into the rooms after hours. She did promise him that if Charlene hadn't returned she would clean the room and contact him if she found anything. Jb walked back to the car to let Divine know what was up "Yo home girl over there said that my mom's left with some young dude the other day and hasn't been back since, she said the nigga had a nice car and that my mom's didn't look right when she was leaving. By the look on Jb's face Divine could tell that he was worried about Charlene. Divine told Jb to follow up with the housekeeper because something didn't smell right. Divine and Jb went back to the crib, when they got in Quan was sleep, Jb headed to bed, Divine knocked out on the couch. The next morning Divine left out early to make a few runs he stopped by to check on his mom's then he went over to see Ace since he really hadn't checked him in a while. "What up D? Ace asked as Divine walked in. Divine sat down on the couch and began to fill Ace in on everything that was going on. "The money is going good but my nigga Jb, a little fucked up right now over his mom's. He hasn't talked to her in a few days. We went by the telly she was staying at and found out she hasn't been there in a few days. The last time anyone saw her she was leaving with some young dude, so I don't know what the fuck is going on." Ace listened and Divine continued on, "Now he just waiting for word from the housekeeper she's going to call him when she cleans the room." Divine asked Ace to put his ear to the streets and let him know if he finds out anything when he told Ace, Jb's mother name was Charlene. Ace paused and said, "I knew a Charlene a long time ago pretty ass young thing too but that's a whole different story I'll keep an ear open and I'll let you know if I hear anything." Divine thanked Ace in advance and headed back to the block. When Jb got back in the crib, Quan was in his room on some quiet shit. He kept trying to get Charlene on the phone, and still couldn't get her. Now he was starting to get pissed because she wasn't calling him and he wasn't getting an answer when he called her. Divine walked in and let Jb know that he had put word out on the street. Jb let him know that he still couldn't get in touch with Charlene. Quan overheard the two of them talking and came outta his room. "What the fuck is y'all doing? "It's called work nigga! Divine replied sarcastically. Jb looked over at Quan and let him know what was going on "shit I'm trying to get in touch with mom dukes she not answering her phone not hitting me back. I went to the telly she was at and nobody hasn't seen her shit is smelling real funky right now." Quan played his part well he showed concern but not too much. He kept his game face on. He knew eventually he would have to deal with Jb. He quickly tried to change the subject by inviting Divine and Jb out to the club to chill and get their mind off the crazy shit. Jb wasn't in the mood to deal with the club scene, but Divine decided to go it had been a long time since they had been to the club.

****

Quan and Divine had decided to go to a new club that had just opened up. The music was bumping as they walked up, there were a few haters standing on the side watching and they breezed through security. Every female in the club single or not, wanted to be around them. Whatever was the hottest drink in the club was Quan always made sure he had it. Quan loved the club because he enjoyed how the females would show off when they knew a nigga with major paper was in the club. He could always spot the naive ones from the bunch and would prey on them all night. Divine on the other hand kept a low profile in the club he would mingle with the ladies, every now and then but most of the time he would just sit back and observe. Damn near every female in the club wanted to leave with Divine he was fine as hell, he had money, and in the hood, that was like hitting the jackpot. Quan and divine left the club around five in the morning and headed back to the crib to get some rest.

A few days had passed and there was still no word from Charlene. Jb got a message from the housekeeper at the hotel that it was urgent for him to come up there, Jb hopped in his car and headed up to the hotel, when he pulled up he noticed the cops were talking to the housekeeper.

 The housekeeper pulled Jb to the side and told him what she saw when she opened up the room door. There was blood on the Dresser, bed and the shower curtain. She even noticed and that Charlene's things and pocket book were still in the room. Jb tried to enter the room but the cops would not let him. As he stood by the door trying to get a look at the inside of the room an detective walked over and told him he needed to go down to the station for questioning. Jb started to flip out. "Why the fuck do I need to come down to the station I'm trying to find my mother! Jb wasn't too eager to go down to the station but the detective insisted that he at least go down and file a missing person's report. He didn't want to have nothing to do with the police at all, and sure as hell didn't need them knowing his business. The detective gave Jb his card and asked him to call him in a few days. While the detectives were waiting for the forensics to arrive, the housekeeper signaled for Jb to meet her on the side of the building. She pulled out an envelope with his name on it and told him she found it on the side of the bed. The cops were so busy looking at everything else they didn't notice the housekeeper give Jb the envelope. Jb took the envelope and walked back to his car before he could open the envelope his phone rung, it was Divine. "What up JB? "Yo D I was going to call you but I'm fucked up right now I'm leaving the telly they found blood in my mom's room and her shit was still in there" Jb was trying to hold himself together as he told Divine to meet him downtown. Divine grabbed his gun and told Jb he would meet him shortly. Divine rushed out the house but before he went downtown to meet up with Jb he stopped by Ace's crib to let him know what Jb had just told him and to see if he heard anything.

Ace was waiting for Divine because he had some very interesting information for him. When Ace had put the word out about Charlene one of his girl's told him she had met a Charlene and the hotel she used for her tricks. She remembered the name because she spoke to her a few times outside of the hotel and found out she was turning tricks for coke. The last time she saw her she was getting into a badass car with a young dude who looked like he had some major paper. Divine made a mental note of the information he was giving and rushed out the door to meet Jb downtown. Jb sat in the car waiting for Divine to arrive. He was so heated by what he saw in Charlene's room that he totally forgot about the letter the housekeeper gave him. Divine pulled up behind Jb's car and walked over to see what was up. "Any more word, on your mom's? Divine asked as he got in the car. "Naw man I'm sitting here trying to figure out what the fuck happened" Jb replied as he banged on his steering wheel. "Well look I did some asking around and found out there was a dude with a nice whip leaving the hotel with her, I also found out Charlene was sniffing coke too." Jb looked at Divine in disbelief, "what nigga, where the fuck you did you hear that from? Divine knew Jb didn't want to hear his mother was a coke head but he gave him the details anyway. "Remember the pimp nigga, well one of his girls was working that area and just so happen her and your mom's had spoken a few times. She put me up on some shit." Jb shook his head and said, "Damn, I'm not even going to think the worst" Divine placed his gun on the dashboard and said, "Nigga the worst is already here. Now we have to deal with it, and we are going to deal with whoever the nigga is that was last seen with her."

Jb and Divine headed to crib to put Quan up on what had happened. "Yo Quan some crazy shit is going down and we need to handle it real quick" not sure what Jb and Divine was talking about Quan asks, "What the fuck happened? Jb starts to give Quan the run down, "Yo they went up in the room and found blood everywhere but my mom's wasn't there, then them fucking blue boys wanted me to come down to the station. You know I wasn't with that shit" Quan listened on as Jb and Divine told him everything that went down at the hotel. He kept his cool as he offered his assistance with finding out what happened. He needed to get out of town for a few days so he made up some bullshit story about Raymond getting into some beef and needed him to come up. Quan grabbed some clothes and headed to Philly. The next day Jb drove back by the hotel to see if he could find out any more information. When he pulled up he saw the housekeeper, he ran up too her asking her more info, she couldn't tell him anything more than what she already did. She wanted to know if he read the letter, Jb had forgotten all about the letter he ran to his car and checked the glove box and there it was. Before he could read it, the housekeeper tapped on the window and distracted him. She told him that the police wanted him to contact them as soon as possible. Jb called the number on the card. "Hello, Detective Bryant This is Jb I'm calling to find out if you have any information on my mother Charlene Jenkins" the detective requested that Jb come in to speak with him personally. Jb agreed, even though he wasn't trying to be caught in a police department but he knew there was a chance the detective had a lead. He drove to the police department; he still hadn't read the letter. Once at the police dept. the detective began to question him.

Jb was getting upset because he knew he didn't have anything to do with what had happened. The detective was talking to him as if he was a suspect. Detective Bryant told Jb there was two different blood types collected from the room and there was semen on the bed. Detective Bryant asked Jb was Charlene involved in Prostitution. Jb stood up "Are you trying to call my mother a hoe? In the back of his mind, he remembered what Divine had told him but he wasn't trying to believe it. Detective Bryant replied, "I'll take that as a no, we'll need to keep in touch with you because this case will be open until we find her or sad to say her body. Jb walked out of the police station angry and confused. Shit wasn't adding up. he decided to drive around and clear his mind. He drove by the restaurant that he and Charlene had went to eat. He sat outside of the restaurant for a while thinking about Charlene as he looked over in the passenger seat he saw the letter the housekeeper had gave him. He finally opened the letter and started to read it.

"Dear Jb,

if you are reading this letter than I know that I am in trouble. I should have sat you down, talked to you, and told you everything. I was afraid that you would judge me; my intentions when I came to New York were not to be a mother to you. I came for all the wrong reasons. a while back when you guys were out I went into Quan's room and I was wrong to do so and I have paid for it ever since that day. I found some coke in his room, I got high, and it started becoming a habit. The second time I did it, he caught me in his room. He was upset and he raped me and made me leave the apartment. He told me to go back home. I didn't I went to a hotel and he found me he raped me over and over and then he put me on a bus and watched me leave but I got off a few stops and came back to get even with him but if your reading this letter I guess I was successful. I love you and I'm sorry love always Charlene."

Jb crumbled the letter as tears rolled down his face he couldn't believe what he just read. The thought that "Quan" his nigga from way back did what he did to his mother was straight grimy. Jb couldn't even think straight he wanted to get at Quan in the worst way but Quan was still in Philly. He called Divine to put him on. "Yo D what up, I need to meet with you ASAP we have a problem, Meet me at the restaurant by the bridge nigga and don't mention anything to that nigga Quan if you talk to him" Divine grabbed his heat and an extra clip. He could tell by Jb's tone that he was in war mode. "It's like that? Divine asked as he headed out the door. Jb replied, "It's like that nigga" and hung up the phone. Divine didn't take long to meet up with Jb. Once he pulled up, he knew by the look on Jb face that some shit was bout to go down. "What's up? Divine asked as he got in the car. "Read this fucking letter than ask me that again" Jb said as he passed Divine the letter. Divine began reading the letter and couldn't believe it. "That nigga Quan couldn't have done that shit" Divine said as he gave the letter back to Jb. "why the fuck would she lie D? Jb said as he pulled his gun from his holster. He was convinced

Quan had something to do with Charlene's disappearance. Divine could tell he was pissed and tried to get him to think everything over. "I'm saying Quan is a fucked up nigga at times. I just can't see him doing no wild shit like that to your mom's. Let's ride back over to the hotel and ask the housekeeper to describe the car she saw your mom get in". Jb put his gun away and drove over to the hotel. When they pulled up to the telly, the housekeeper was busy cleaning rooms. Jb waited til she was finished and asked her if she remembered the color of the car. She told him the car was green. That right there was exactly what Jb and Divine didn't want to hear because Quan's car was green. Everybody in the hood called it the making money monster. Divine wanted to double check on the info he had got from Ace, he called him up and asked him to with his girls about the color of the car. "Yo Ace ask your girls if they remember the color of that car? Ace called out to one of his girls and one of them told him the car was green. Divine hung up the phone and looked at Jb knowing that it was no way that two different people would give the same color of the car. Divine told Jb what Ace had told him, the colors of the car were a match. Divine looked at Jb and said, "So what's up you want to go at this nigga with this info we got and check his story or you want to wait? Jb cocked his gun back and said, "right now I want to take it to this nigga but I want to know where she is and what's up first before I do anything" Divine and Jb decided they both would keep what they found out on the hush until the time was right to confront Quan. Quan was still in Philly but he called to let them know he would be back on the weekend. The next day Jb checked his messages, still no word from Charlene he was starting to realize he wasn't going to hear from her at all.

He sat on the couch and began flicking through the channels. He stopped on the local news channel. The story caught his attention.

"Police in upstate New York have found a woman's body floating in a stream. The woman has yet to be identified but police have reported that she is African American." Jb didn't really think anything of it as he turned away from the channel. Divine was awakened by his cellphone ringing, it was business as usual, he told Jb they needed to go pick up some work. Divine and Jb headed to meet with the connect to pick up some work, even though it was drama within the team that didn't stop them from making money.

****

A few weeks had past and the body of the woman found in upstate New York was still unidentified. Detective Bryant had heard about the story and decided to take a ride upstate to see if the woman was Charlene. he didn't want to contact Jb until he knew for sure. After speaking with local authorities and feeling like he had a lead, he decided to go ahead and contact Jb to have him come up and view the body. Jb got the call from Detective Bryant and directions, and then he and Divine got on the road to go view the body. While they were driving, Jb hoped and prayed it wasn't his mother. After a few hours of driving, they finally arrived at the morgue. Jb took a deep breath, and then walked in to meet Detective Bryant. Divine decided to stay in the lobby while Jb and Detective Bryant walked into the morgue to view the body. The coroner unzipped the body bag and Jb broke down as he looked at the lifeless body on the table. He identified the woman as his mother Charlene Jenkins. Tears filled his eyes as he stormed out of the morgue. Divine was outside when he saw Jb walking out. He knew by Jb's face that it had to be Charlene. "Damn J it was your mom's? Divine asked as he tried to console Jb.

Wiping his face Jb replied. "Why the fuck did that nigga do that shit? Detective Bryant walked out and overheard Jb and Divine talking. He walked over and asked, "Do you know who did this Jb? Jb didn't play the snitch game and he wanted to handle Quan himself. He decided not to tell detective Bryant anything about Quan or the letter that Charlene had wrote him. He replied firmly. "No I don't know who did this but I wish I did." Detective Bryant looked at Jb and said, "Well son that's my job, just let us handle this and we will find the bastard that did this. It will be an autopsy done to determine the exact cause of death and I will contact you with the results." Jb walked to the car with his mind set on dealing with Quan. on the drive back to the city neither Jb or Divine spoke a word. Divine knew that Jb wanted to get at Quan and he wasn't going to stop him neither but he never thought in a million years the empire they worked so hard to build would crumble on the count of a nigga in their crew. Meanwhile up in Philly Quan was unaware of what Jb had just found out he was getting himself together to get ready for the drive back. Once back in the hood Jb went to the crib to focus on his plan to deal with Quan. He told Divine that when Quan got back he was going to kill him, Divine wasn't going to stop Quan at all but he advised him to make sure when he made his move he made it right.

****

Up in Philly Quan had told Raymond what he did, and how he was planning on dealing with Jb. Raymond knew that if Quan succeeded that he would be getting way more paper than what he was getting doing the kick in the door bullshit. He offered to go back to New York with Quan to handle the situation, but Quan told him he could handle himself.

He was planning on dealing with Jb before the shit hit the fan; little did he know it already had. Raymond wasn't worried about Quan but he wanted to know what was going to do about Divine, since it seemed him and Jb was on some batman and robin shit. Quan looked at his cousin and said; " oh I got some shit planned for him as if one go down they both going down" Raymond gave Quan a pound and replied " I feel you on that nigga" Quan told Raymond he would get in touch with him after he dealt with the situation. Quan hopped in his car and headed back to the city, he was dead set on getting at Jb. Meanwhile back at the crib Jb was trying to think back to every time Charlene was at the crib to see if he missed any signs, wondering if he could have prevented what happened. Divine went back over to Ace's crib to let him know what happened. As he walked in, he asked Ace had he been watching the news. Ace didn't really watch the news. Divine sat down and told him that Jb's mother body was found floating in a stream. Ace couldn't believe what he was hearing. Ace asked how Jb was holding up and Divine told him that Jb was feeling fucked up. "Any word on who did it? Ace asked, Divine looked at Ace with a serious face and said, "You wouldn't believe it if I told you man" Ace eyes widened as he said "hell no not a nigga y'all knew! Divine shook his head and said, "Our right hand nigga! "Damn" Ace said as he shook his head in disbelief. "What was her name again? Ace asked. "Charlene Jenkins" Divine replied. Ace wanted to know where she was from. Divine explained how she had lived in New York when she was younger and then moved down south. A few years after she moved she sent Jb to live with his grandmother. Ace listened closely as Divine spoke about Charlene. Her name kept ringing bells in his head. Divine noticed Ace had a weird look on his face. Ace told him he had a weird feeling but he had to make a few calls first. Divine decided to head back to the crib to check on Jb. Ace sat on the couch wondering if Charlene Jenkins was the same Charlene he had knew. He pulled out one of his old photo albums and found a picture of the Charlene that he had been in love with a long time ago. He decided to make a few calls to some old friends that he dealt with around that time to see if anyone of them remembered Charlene.

****

Divine pulled up to the crib and noticed Quan was arriving at the same time. He kept his cool as he walked over to Quan's car. As bad as he wanted to call Jb and tell him Quan was on his upstairs, he knew it would look suspicious. As they walked, Divine signaled Jb to keep his cool. Jb held in his anger as he gave Quan and Divine a pound. Quan sat back on the couch and rolled a blunt and asked Jb if he wanted to smoke. Jb told Quan he would smoke a little later. He decided to fuck with Quan's head a little bit to see what kind of reaction he could get from him. " this broad I was fucking with just wrote me talking bout she pregnant and shit" Quan looked up from rolling his blunt "better get that a-1 special nigga" Jb replied, "Naw shorty talking bout she like 7 months" Quan laughed and said; "well nigga looks like you going to be a fucking daddy". Jb pulled his gun out, put in on the counter, and said, "Fuck that I'm going to kill that bitch! Quan put the blunt down and looked at Jb thinking to himself why did he just say that shit. Wondering if Jb knew what he had done. "No fucking way" he thought to himself. He knew Jb would have shot him as soon as he walked in the door. Quan busted out laughing as he sparked his blunt. "You crazy as hell Jb". Divine really couldn't tell what direction the night was going was go to go in. Jb didn't give him any sign that he wanted to take care of Quan right then and there, so he sat back on the couch and dozed off. Quan and Jb sat up smoking. Quan was high and wanted to go to a strip club; he asked Jb if he wanted to go, Jb wasn't sure if Quan was trying to get him out the house on some sneaky shit or if he really wanted to go to a strip club. He told Quan he was going to the store then heading to bed. Quan went in his room to get right for the club while Jb went to the store, he wanted to get at Quan badly but he needed the right moment and he wanted Divine to be close by. Once back upstairs Jb noticed that Quan was gone, and Divine was awake. "Yo what the fuck happened? Divine as he wondered what he had missed while he was sleep. "That nigga went to the tittie club and I went to the store." Jb said as he showed Jb his bag of goodies. "I know you wasn't going to handle that shit tonight" Divine said as he got up from the couch. Jb pulled his gun out and said, " trust me, I'm going to get at that nigga but I gotta do that shit away from the crib, it's burning me up to even be around this nigga". Divine looked at Jb's face and knew he was dead set on dealing with Quan. "I thought you were going to beat the nigga ass when we walked in the crib." Divine and Jb sat up getting the plan right while Quan was enjoying himself at the club. After a few hours, Quan finally made it back to the crib. Jb and Divine were sleep went he got in; he was so drunk he didn't even realize he could have popped Divine and Jb right then and there. The next morning Jb received a call from Detective Bryant asking him to come to the station. Once he arrived at the station; Detective Bryant told him the exact cause of Charlene's death and that he was still looking for the suspect. Jb called Divine to let him know what he had found out, while he was on the phone with Jb Quan walked in. Divine quickly changed the subject to give him a clue that Quan was listening. "I guess you better take her to handle that real soon." As Divine was hanging up the phone, Quan asked him what was going on with Jb. "that nigga said shorty wilding talking bout she keeping the baby." Quan still didn't have a clue that Divine and Jb were on to his ass, either way he was still planning to deal with Jb real soon. Divine told Quan it was work that needed to be picked up. Quan decided he would make the trip and asked if Jb or Divine would be coming with him, Divine told him that he would check with Jb to see what he wanted to do. Quan was hoping that Divine would stay at the crib and Jb would go with him that would allow him to get the work and handle Jb. Divine called Jb on the phone to see where he was. "Yo Jb, where you at? Jb answered in an upset tone; "man I'm at the fucking shop, I was driving back to the crib and my shit just started smoking." Divine grabbed his keys and told Jb he would come pick him up. "Damn" said Divine and he started to walk out the door. Before he could leave Quan asked him what happened he told Quan that he had to go pick Jb up from the car shop. Divine headed out the door to get Jb. On the way, back to the crib Divine told Jb they needed to go make a pick up later and that Quan was going. Jb told Divine that he would handle Quan later on that night. Divine respected Jb's decision but advised him that they would handle business first. Later on that night Divine, Jb and Quan were getting ready to go take care of business, when Divine got a call unexpected call from Ace. Divine could tell by the tone of Ace's voice that something was bothering him. Ace told Divine that he needed him to get over to his crib as soon as possible and what he had to tell him he needed to tell him in person. Divine wasn't sure what Ace needed to talk to him about, he just knew it was important. Divine told Ace he would be there after he handled his business but Ace insisted he come now because it was about Jb's mother. Divine told Jb and Quan to go ahead without him, and he would meet up with them later. he didn't really feel comfortable sending Jb alone with Quan because he knew he wasn't sure if Jb was going to deal with Quan before he met up with them. Divine gave Jb a signal to wait for him before he did anything, Quan was too busy with his own plotting to even notice. Divine drove off in one direction to go see Ace, while Quan and Jb headed in the opposite direction to go to the pick-up location.

There can only be one chapter 6

On the way to the pick-up location Jb really didn't speak much he was focused on dealing with Quan. He tried to block Charlene out his mind because he didn't want to get emotional in front of Quan. Quan was blasting his radio acting as if nothing was wrong. Each of them knew the other one was strapped. Number one rule in the hood never handle business without your heat. Before they arrived at the pick-up location, Quan told Jb he had to make a stop. Jb wasn't feeling the detour but he didn't have any choice he wasn't in his car. Quan pulled his car over on the side of the road claiming he had to piss. Jb told him to make it quick because they couldn't afford to be a minute late, Jb didn't suspect anything as he waited for Quan to return to the car. Jb he called Divine to let him know what was up, Divine told him to keep his cool until he was able to get there, Jb agreed and hung up the phone. Quan walked back to the car and was ready to go. They made it to the pick-up location, handled business and everything went smooth. As they were headed to meet up with Divine, Quan slowed down the car claiming something was wrong and he needed to check under the hood to make sure everything was ok. Quan got out of the car, and popped the hood and begin to check under it. Jb sat in the car for a few minutes then rolled down the window to ask Quan if everything was good. Quan told him that the oil was low, and asked Jb to look in the trunk to see if he saw a container of oil. Quan knew exactly what he was doing, he checked to make sure no cars were passing by, pulled his gun from the holster, and took the safety off. Jb walked to the back of the car to check for the oil. All he saw in the trunk was the work they picked up and some empty sneaker boxes and a gas can. He yelled to the front of the car, "I don't see any oil back here, so I guess you outta luck nigga" Still bent down looking in the trunk he didn't even see Quan creeping on the other side of the car. Quan placed the gun to Jb's side and said. "no nigga I think you're outta luck." Jb was caught totally off guard before he could reach for his gun; Quan shot him in his side. Jb took off running through the woods he could not believe Quan just shot him. Quan ran after him trying to get a few more shots in but kept missing. Quan turned around and ran back to his car. Jb knew it wasn't over; he grabbed his phone from his pocket and called Divine. "Yo D, this nigga just shot me, this nigga just fucking shot me! Divine could barely hear him from all the static in the phone. Divine kept yelling though the phone as Jb tried to get a better reception, it wasn't working and his cell battery was dying. Jb yelled through the phone "Quan nigga" Then his phone went dead. He tried to look for a pay phone or someone driving by. He was on a dark as road and there was no cars driving by. Jb figured he could make it up the road he might find a gas station as he was walking; a car came speeding up the road. The fog lights were on so he couldn't see the driver of the car. Quan sped up alongside Jb and started shooting at him, Jb pulled his gun out and tried to shoot back but Quan shot him in his head. Once he saw Jb's body hit the ground, Quan put the car in park and quickly went into the trunk and pulled the gas can. He poured the gas on Jb's body and lit a match before he set Jb's body on fire he stood over him and said, "Now you can join that hoe ass mother of yours." Quan dropped the match, returned to his car, and drove off.

Quan had no idea that Jb had called Divine and told him what he had done. Divine was bugging by the phone call he just got from Jb. He kept trying to call Jb back but he got the box. He was pulling up to Ace's crib when Jb called him after the phone call dropped he decided to make a U-turn and go to the crib and get some more bullets. While driving, Quan called up one of his jump-offs for a favor. Quan told her he would break her off if she did exactly what he asked her to do. He asked to meet him in 45 minutes and she agreed. Quan picked her up as planned and gave her strict instructions on what he needed her to do. His plan was to get her to drop a few dimes on Divine. As they got closer to the precinct, he gave her the run down. "I want you to go down to the precinct and tell them that you use to fuck with my nigga Divine. Tell them that he's abusive, a drug dealer and that you overheard him one night bragging how he killed a woman want to know and then give them the address to the crib." The female wasn't too happy with what Quan was asking her to do, she didn't even want to know why he was asking her to set his boy up and since but he promised to pay her lovely she agreed to do what he had asked. Quan pulled up to the precinct and told her to make sure she stuck to the script. He told her he would drive around the block until he saw her come back out. Quan drove up a few blocks, called Raymond and told him to pack a few bags and meet him in a few hours down the block from his crib. Raymond knew by Quan's tone that some shit had gone down; he didn't bother to asks for details he hung up the phone and started packing. Quan waited a few minutes and then texted his Jump off and told her something came up and he had to go. He told her to take a cab and meet him at his crib when she was finished.

Quan headed to the crib to grab the majority of his things from the crib, he took all his clothes and anything else that could fit into bags, including the money from the safe. An hour had passed and Raymond called him and told him that he would be arriving shortly. Meanwhile Divine drove to a few hospitals to see if Jb was in the E.R. every hospital he checked he was told Jb wasn't there. Divine drove around hoping that Jb would get in touch with him. Quan was finished removing his things from the apartment. The jump off called him and told him she was finished and on her way to meet him. Quan called Raymond and told him to stay in the car when he got there. A few minutes passed by and the jump off was knocking on the door, Quan let her in and rolled a blunt for them to smoke. She told him the police told her they would be making a trip soon to check out the information she had giving them. Quan took a few pulls of the blunt to get his mind right. He walked over to the stereo and turned the volume up and walked into his room and got a pillow, when he walked back into the living room and charged at the jump off and shot her three times. He picked the slugs up from the floor, put the pillow in a garbage bag, ripped open a few bags of coke and sprinkled them around the room. He wiped everything he touched in the crib and headed out the door. Raymond was waiting down stairs, Quan walked to the car and put his bags in and told Raymond to follow him. Quan drove across town to a chop shop to get rid of his car. When he was finished he got into Raymond's car and told him that he had took care of Jb and Divine. Raymond knew this day was coming and he mentally prepared himself. Quan told him to stop at a gas station to fill up the tank because they were taking a trip down south.

Divine was getting tired of driving around and decided to head back to the crib. As he walked in, he noticed a woman slouched on the couch, before he could walk over to check on her, he heard a banging on the door. Assuming it was Jb he hurried and open the door, to his surprise it was the police "Damn" Divine thought to himself as the cops walked in, one of the officers noticed the body slouched on the couch was the female who had just been in the precinct filing a report against Divine. The officer rushed over to the couch to check on the female, her body was cold. "Divine Williams you are under arrest! The officer said as he wrestled Divine to the floor. "Hold the fuck up! Divine yelled as the officers placed the cuffs on him. He knew he was fucked, he was caught in an apartment with a dead body, and the fucking cops weren't trying to hear shit he had to say. As the officers escorted Divine out of the apartment, everybody on the blocked stared at Divine, trying to figure what he had done. The officers placed Divine in the car and took him down to the precinct. Six hours had gone by in the interrogation room and Divine was getting tired of answering the same questions. When he refused to answer any more of the officer's questions, he was processed and placed in a cell. Divine knew that Quan had a whole lot to do with him being in there, but he still didn't know where Jb was. He sat in the cell hoping that Jb was safe.

****

Quan and Raymond were still on the road heading down south. Quan knew before the night was over Divine would be in jail. Quan had done what he set out to do, Jb was dead and Divine was out of the way.

The next day Divine's face was all over the news and in the papers. Ace had heard from one of his girl's, that Divine was in jail. Ace knew that Divine was innocent. Ace wanted to speak to Divine directly but he wasn't too excited with the thought of speaking with him at the jail. He had one of his girls call the jail and get the address and visiting information. Champagne was down for anything when it came to Ace. Out of all of the girls, she was the only one that he didn't sleep with. Ace treated her different she was more like his pet instead of hoe. He never made her do anything she didn't want to do. Ace had met Champagne a year earlier, when they met; she was just "Keisha" a naive girl who fell for the wrong guy. Keisha had come to New York with a guy she had met back home in Texas. He promised her the world and gassed her up to go back to New York with him. Keisha had never been outside of Texas, so the thought of going somewhere else especially New York enticed her. Once she got to New York with him, he got what he wanted from her and kicked her to the curb. Homeless and clueless she found herself on the streets of New York begging for change to get by. She walked in a diner one morning to get something to eat and that's when she met Infinity. Infinity was Ace's bottom Bitch; she had been with him since the age of 16. Her mother introduced her to the game early on. She was a cold-hearted female who didn't give a fuck about anything but money. She would go out, find girls, and talk them into coming home with her. Infinity walked in the diner and noticed Keisha sitting at a table. She was eating as if she hadn't had a meal in a very long time. "Damn" Infinity thought to herself as she looked on in disgust. Infinity ordered some food and sat down. She kept staring at Keisha as she watched her demolish her food. She could tell by the condition of Keisha's clothing that she was in a fucked up situation. Infinity walked over to the table where Keisha was sitting at and placed a five-dollar bill on the table. Keisha quickly grabbed the money from the table and told Infinity thank you. Infinity could tell by Keisha's accent that she wasn't from out of town. Infinity set her sights on getting another moneymaker for Ace. Infinity's food was ready; she grabbed it and walked back over to Keisha's table. "Where you from? She asked as she sat down. Keisha looked up at her and replied; "Texas" Infinity laughed at the way Keisha pronounced Texas. "Damn you talk funny, what the fuck you doing all the way up here? Infinity asked as she looked down at Keisha's shoes. Keisha said, "It's a long story but I'm trying to get home, but I don't have the money for a ticket" Infinity knew it would be easy to Keisha to leave with her after hearing that. She told Keisha that she knew where she could get some quick money to get back home; little did Keisha know it required having sex for money. Not having a place to stay or any money, Keisha agreed to go with Infinity. They left the diner and headed straight to Ace's crib; before they got there, Infinity called Ace and told him she had a present for him. He knew exactly what that meant, "another money maker." When Keisha walked in with Infinity as soon as Keisha walked in with Infinity, Ace looked at her in a way he had never looked at any of the other girls. He could tell she didn't have a clue what she was getting herself into. Infinity took her in the back to get cleaned up and gave her a few outfits to try on. Keisha was getting the Infinity makeover. When Infinity was done she walked Keisha back out into the living room and Ace was impressed by what Infinity had done.

Keisha looked beautiful, the dress she had on went well with her honey brown complexion and hazel eyes. Ace gave her the name "Champagne" because he thought the name suited her well. He pulled Infinity to the side and told her to teach Keisha well. Infinity knew what she had to do but she also knew she had to stay on top of her game because she sure as hell wasn't going to let some lil bitch from Texas steal her shine away from her. Infinity worked hard teaching Keisha the code of the streets, how to walk what and what not to wear, who and who not to talk too. Keisha didn't ask questions she was happy she had a pace to stay and got to wear nice things. A few weeks went by and it was time for Keisha to hit the track. The first night Keisha was nervous but Infinity told her she didn't have anything to worry about she would be right there with her. The tricks were pulling up back to back, each one interested in the new girl. After her first sexual encounter, Keisha was starting to get into the swing of things and since the men were paying her, the street life didn't bother her. She was no longer Keisha that girl was dead and gone; Champagne was getting money, and loving it.

****

Champagne called the jail and got all of Divine's info, she wrote him a letter letting him know she needed to see him. When Divine read the letter he knew exactly who she was and that she was most likely coming with a message from Ace. On visiting day, Divine waited for Champagne to arrive. Once she got there, she told Divine that Ace believed he was innocent and he had his back. Champagne told Divine to use the post office address she had wrote him from and send a letter to Ace telling him what he needed done. Divine wanted to speak to Ace directly but he decided he wait until he was transferred to ask Ace to visit him. Weeks had past and the streets were still talking about Divine being arrested. Charlene was buried and there still was no word on Jb. Divine didn't have a bond and did not want a court appointed attorney, he knew he needed a paid lawyer if he stood a chance to beat the charges. Sitting in his cell, he remembered Jeremiah, and that he was in law school. Divine didn't have a number for him so he called Champagne and asked her to look him up. After a few days of searching for Jeremiah's information Champagne found it, she wrote his information down and mailed it to Divine. Divine wasn't sure if Jeremiah would be able to represent him and if he could, would he be willing to. Divine wrote a letter to Jeremiah requesting his legal services. It took two weeks before he received a response, not only was Jeremiah a defense attorney but he agreed to represent him. A few days later Jeremiah made a visit to the jail to speak to Divine about his case. "Good afternoon, Mr. Williams I am Jeremiah Richards and I'll be your attorney" my name is Jeremiah Richards and I'll be your attorney." Divine wasn't sure if Jeremiah recognized him, in the letter he had written he didn't mention anything about their past. He decided to keep his cool and wait until Jeremiah said something first. Jeremiah knew who Divine was as soon as he received his letter he had only met one Divine in his lifetime, he wasn't sure if Divine was guilty or innocent but either way Divine was his friend. Jeremiah kept it professional during the visit speaking only about the case. Based on the charges, Divine would be facing some years if found guilty. Divine was being charge with Charlene's murder along with the murder of the female in his apartment. The drug charge didn't stick, since it wasn't any drugs found in the apartment other than what Quan had sprinkled around. Jeremiah sat in the visiting reviewing the case files, something just wasn't adding up. Jeremiah slipped him a note; "I reviewed everything in this case and something just doesn't add up. I know we haven't kicked in years but I am going to help you beat this." Divine looked up at Jeremiah after reading the note and he knew he had done the right thing by asking Jeremiah to represent him. Divine gave Jeremiah the note and thanked him. The visit was over and Divine returned to his cell. He needed to get a letter out to Ace to let him know what was going on. In the letter, he wrote Ace, he asked Ace to put his ears to the streets and get any information he could on Jb and on Quan. He also told Ace that he knew that Quan set him up. Divine sent the letter out and waited to hear from Ace, he knew Ace would most likely send Champagne up to the jail to give him information. Ace got the letter and immediately put the word out. The streets weren't talking that much no one had seen Jb and Quan whereabouts weren't known. Jeremiah came to visit Divine a few days later and had some good news. Based on the evidence the homicide team pulled from the Charlene Jenkins case Divine's dna did not match. He was still being charged with the murder of the female who was found in his apartment. Jeremiah told Divine that if could give the cops another suspect, he could walk out of there a free man. Divine wasn't with the snitch movement and he wasn't falling for the get out jail free bullshit. He would deal with Quan himself and without the cops involved. Jeremiah asked Divine where Jb was at and Divine told him what had happen the night he was locked up, and how he was worried that Quan may have killed Jb as well.

Jeremiah couldn't believe what he was hearing but for the most part he couldn't believe that once associated with a murderer. Jeremiah told Divine to make sure he was completely honest with him and didn't leave anything out. Because once he went to trial, he didn't want to look like a asshole if the prosecutor pulled up information that Jeremiah wasn't aware of. Divine wanted to be sure he heard Jeremiah correctly "did you just say father in law? Jeremiah nodded his head letting Divine know he had heard him correctly, he was engaged to the judge's daughter. Divine couldn't believe what Jeremiah had just told him. He wasn't sure if that was going to work for him or against him. He sat in his cell thinking about his case, his mother and the streets, he knew Jb was a lost cause he couldn't be alive or he would have sent word to him all he remembered was Jb calling him saying Quan shot him. A few weeks went by and Divine transferred to another facility. Ace decided it was time for him to visit him. Divine was a little more comfortable at the new facility, he was able to receive contact visits instead of talking to his visitors through a glass. on visitation day Divine waited for Ace to arrive; once Ace arrived he told Divine that he heard the female found in the apartment had been to the precinct earlier that night dropping a dime on Divine. Right then Divine had confirmation that Quan had really went out of his way to set him up. Divine asked Ace to send someone to check on his mother, he wanted to make sure she was holding up ok. He knew that most likely she was stressing over him being in jail. Ace told Divine not to worry he would send one of his girl's over there to check on her. Divine told Ace to make sure whomever he sent over there looked right he didn't want them to give his mother the wrong idea. Ace agreed and told Divine

Not to worry whomever he decided to send would play the role of his girlfriend. Before the visit was over Ace remembered that he never got to tell Divine what he need to tell him the night everything happened.

"Man you ain't going to believe this shit but I use to deal with Charlene a long time ago." Divine looked at Ace surprised by what he had just said. "What nigga, how long ago" Divine was trying to match Ace's information with Jb's age. "It was a long time she was young and her mother did couldn't stand me of course I was much older than her but I really loved that girl!" Ace said as a tear rolled down his face. Divine could tell that Ace was serious; he asked Ace was he Jb's father. Ace told him that he didn't think it was possible because when him and Charlene were together she never mentioned anything about being pregnant. They messed around for a year and next thing he knew she had moved. The visit was over and Ace promised Divine that he would be back soon. Divine walked back to his cell, he couldn't believe that Ace knew Charlene and that they once were a couple. He wondered if there was a chance that Ace was Jb's father. Divine didn't dwell on it too much he needed to focus on his case.

****

Denise hadn't heard from her son at all. She couldn't believe that he was being charged with murder. She wanted to see Divine but she couldn't pull herself to visit her son in jail. It was bad enough everyone that knew her were already passing judgment. However, Denise still held her head high she knew she didn't raise a murderer. She sat in room looking through old photo albums at Divine's pictures when he was younger. Divine was a happy child, well behaved in school and very smart.

Denise always kept her son Dressed well, she worked hard to give him everything he needed. She couldn't see where she went wrong, was it the influence of growing up without a father. She questioned many things but she didn't question the way she raised her son. It had been a week since Divine had any visits; Champagne sent him a letter to let him know that his mother was okay. Once Divine knew that, he was able to focus on getting out jail. Champagne began to write Divine more and more as time went by most of the times the letters had nothing to do with Ace at all. Champagne started to grow feelings for Divine. She wasn't sure if his feelings were mutual, she was afraid that he wouldn't want to deal with because of who she was. She knew that Ace would not allow it because his number one rule was if it wasn't a money move it wasn't a move at all. Divine started spending a lot of time out of his cell and in the recreation room. After a few conversations he met some dudes from Philly, who just happened to know Raymond and weren't too fond of him. They were two of Raymond's boys who went on robbery sprees with him and didn't get the cut they were owed. They heard about Divine's charges and they heard he was down with G.M.C the name of his crew got one of the dudes attention. He had heard that name before one night out with Raymond. One of them walked over to where Divine was sitting. "you down with that GMC click? Divine stood up and said, "It depends, who wants to know." The dude didn't have a problem with Divine, he replied "ain't no beef nigga the name was floating around in Philly" Divine figured that either knew Quan or Raymond so he asked the dude if he knew Raymond. The dude knew exactly who Divine was talking about. Raymond was the reason they were in there.

Divine listened closely as the dude begins to explain his situation with Raymond. "That nigga shorted us on some bread from a few robberies we did with him. Then he sent us to hit a crib without him, promises us a bigger cut we hit the crib, come outside the car is gone and the cops are pulling up. Shit was a little strange, that nigga ain't been to visit, send no money to a nigga nothing. The fucked up shit is that his sister is my baby mama." Divine listened on, figuring that if he could get to Raymond most likely, he could get to Quan. Then he asked the dude if he had an address for Raymond. The dude from Philly told Divine Raymond wasn't in Philly anymore. Because the last time he talked to his baby mama she told him that Raymond and her cousin went out of town and she didn't think they were coming back. Divine knew the cousin had to be Quan. His plan now was to get dude to get his baby mama to find out Quan's whereabouts. "I need to come to rec more often" Divine gave the dudes a pound and headed back to his cell to soak up the info he just stumbled upon. Divine hoped he would find out Quan's location soon so that he could have him dealt with., he knew Quan wasn't in New York knowing Quan he went somewhere Divine least expect.

****

Quan and Raymond were laying low down south. Quan was enjoying everything from the money to the females. His intentions were to creep back up to New York without being seen. Raymond always had Quan's back with any and everything but he didn't agree with Quan wanted return back to New York. He felt it was too soon and it would be a bad move. Quan felt differently, he felt as if he couldn't be touched. "By now shit should have died down and that nigga should have his time."

Quan said as he tried to convince Raymond that Divine wouldn't be a problem. "I know that nigga D, is locked, but what if this nigga put a word out about you nigga," Raymond asked, hoping that Quan would re-think things. Quan wasn't worried about the cops because he knew Divine wasn't a snitch and he was prepared for nigga that felt like they wanted to bring it to him. Raymond finally agreed to go with Quan and asked, "so when you trying to make that trip? Quan laughed, he knew that Raymond was going to give in and agree with him. "I'll let you know when we're ready for all of that, but right now it's too much money down here and way too much pussy." Quan said as he glanced at some females walking by. That was Quan's weakness; money and bitches. Meanwhile back in New York Divine had let Ace know what he found out about Raymond and Quan. He wasn't ready to set a plan in order. He was still waiting on an exact location for Quan. Divine tried to stay focused on his case, his trial date had not been set yet. Jeremiah was working hard on Divine's case and every time he reviewed the evidence; nothing was adding up. Divine wasn't giving up any names. The cops believed that their case against him was strong enough for a conviction. Jeremiah set his mind on winning this case. Not only for Divine, but also to stick it to his soon to be father in law. The Judge wasn't too fond of Jeremiah or pleased that he was engaged to his daughter. The Judge had heard many negative things about Jeremiah. After law school Jeremiah was engaged to be married to another female and didn't show up at his own wedding. Jeremiah wasn't ready for marriage but his father insisted that he go through with it. His former fiancée was a fellow law student her name was Stephanie Washington.

Stephanie didn't take being stood up at the alter too well. The embarrassment caused her to become very bitter. She was a prosecuting attorney and that worked well since Jeremiah was on the opposite side. She would make sure she was always across the table on any case and her plan was always to win. She even kept score and so far, it was 4 to 2, four wins and two losses. Jeremiah disliked working in the courtroom with her. The remarks she would make after each case pissed him off. The Judge had heard about the two of them but as long as they remained professional in the courtroom, he didn't say anything. However, he warned his daughter Amanda not to make any permanent plans with Jeremiah because he didn't want the same thing to happen to her. Judge Palmer Dobbs would always keep his conversations to a minimum with Jeremiah in the courtroom. Outside the courthouse it was a different story, he would invite Jeremiah to accompany him on the golf course after a few rounds of scotch with his fellow colleagues he would insult Jeremiah continuously. Jeremiah would keep his cool until he got home, then he would vent to Amanda about her father's behavior.

****

"I don't know how much longer I can put up with your father Amanda," Jeremiah said as he walked in pissed off once again by the Judge. "Jeremiah you know that my father has his ways, he's only kidding with you." Amanda tried to lighten the situation. "You call what he's doing kidding? Jeremiah asked as walked over to the refrigerator to grab a beer. "I'll try to talk to him about it." Amanda kissed Jeremiah, she knew her father could say cruel things at times, but that is how he has been since she was younger.

Jeremiah sat down on the couch and opened his briefcase to go over Divine's case. Amanda walked over and asked him about it. "What case are you working on? Jeremiah didn't normally discuss his cases with her but since she seemed interested he told her. "The Divine Williams case" Amanda wanted to know what his client was being charged with. "What did he do? She asked. "Well he's charged with murder" Jeremiah replied. Amanda got up and walked away. She didn't want to hear anything else, she couldn't understand why Jeremiah would want to defend a murderer. Jeremiah couldn't understand why Amanda just walked away. "Where are you going? Did I say something wrong? "You're defending a murderer that's what's wrong! "I am a fucking defense attorney. This is what I do! Jeremiah slammed his briefcase down. He couldn't believe how Amanda was acting. "Please tell me he isn't black" She asked, "what does that have to do with anything? If you must know, he is black! Jeremiah said as he looked at Amanda, waiting for her to say something to push him over the edge. "Oh that explains a lot," Amanda, said with a smirk, "what the hell are you trying to say? Jeremiah didn't like where the conversation was going. Sitting there listening to Amanda, he started to wonder if his soon to be wife was racist. As long as he knew her, he never saw her with any black people but he didn't think she was racist. "I'm just saying this might not look good on us. Jeremiah couldn't believe what she just said. "That's all that you're worried about your snobby ass friends. Fuck the fact that a person, may be sitting in jail for some shit he didn't do." "Why are you raising your voice and talking like a" Amanda paused "like a what? I know you weren't going to say nigger! Jeremiah shook his head, stormed out and decided he would go for a drive to calm down.

Starting to heat up chapter 7

Divine finally received word from Jeremiah that his trial would start in three months. Divine wasn't happy about it but he had no other choice but to wait it out. He was starting to get tired of being behind bars. Besides the once in a blue visits from Ace, all he had to keep him going was his plot for revenge and Champagne's letters. Divine figured out that she was starting to have feelings for him, shit her freaky letters made it obvious enough. Divine wasn't really feeling her, she was fine and all, but he knew how she got down and he wasn't trying to go there with her. Champagne made a surprise visit to see Divine and see what was up with him. "What's up Champagne" Divine made Champagne blush by the way he would say her name. She still answered to champagne but wanted Divine to look at her and see Keisha and not Champagne. "Hey Divine. I told you to call me Keisha," Champagne said as she giggled. "Well excuse me Keisha, so what did Ace send you to tell me this time? Divine thought she was coming with some hood news or something else from Ace. "Actually I came to see you on my own" Divine sat back in the chair and replied "word and why is that? Because I like talking to you, I enjoy these visits and I don't see what everybody else sees, I see someone who just hasn't met the right woman yet" Champagne knew Divine wasn't seeing anyone and if he was they weren't coming to see him. She wanted to prove her feelings to Divine, she looked around slowly to make sure no guards were clocking her as she moved her hand inside of Divine's jump suit and begin playing with his penis. Jerking it up and down. Divine didn't bother to stop her, he enjoyed every minute of it.

Divine whispered as he tried to keep a straight face. "Damn girl, you going to fuck around and get me in trouble." Champagne licked her lips and said, "I know you ain't scared? Divine bit down on his bottom lip to keep from moaning as he busted all over his boxers. He waited a few minutes then walked to the bathroom to wipe off. Champagne sat at the table waiting for him to come back; she wanted to make sure he knew how much she cared for him. As soon as Divine sat down at the table, she decided to get it out the way. "Divine, I know you have a lot on your mind but I really want to know how you feel about me. Divine knew that was coming but he didn't think she would come at him on the spot like that. "Damn you going to lay it on me like that, give a nigga a good nut than hit me with the questions? well you cool people, you fine as hell but right now I'm not trying to be tied down to anyone. I'm cool as hell with Ace and I'm not sure how he would feel about the situation." Champagne hoped that Divine would respond differently towards her but he didn't "well I'm not going to be doing this shit for long I got goals, I'm going to do something more than sell my ass" looking at Champagne's face Divine knew she was serious. He knew she didn't tell Ace because he would have been up there to speak to Divine himself. The visit was over Champagne gave Divine a hug and told him that she would give it all up for him. Divine headed back to his cell. Champagne walked away, he knew she was feeling him but he still wasn't trying to go there with her. He never let any female get too close to him that's why he didn't have most of the problems a lot of niggas had, the baby mama bullshit and the drama. He had problems but they weren't behind no bitch. Champagne headed back to the city she knew she would have some explaining to do, about her visit to Divine. Once back at the house the other girls made it very clear that Ace was upset with Champagne. Infinity made it her business to say something to Champagne. "Damn you riding Divine dick" Champagne could tell Infinity was feeling some kind of way. "What makes you think that? Champagne asked. "Cause every time I turn around you always up there visiting his ass and half of the time you going up there on some square shit." Champagne rolled her eyes as she began to walk down the hall. "Look Infinity I don't have time for this shit where is Ace" "oh now his name is Ace, yeah you really trippin bitch let me find out Divine is your new daddy." Infinity was putting hands all in Champagne's face trying to provoke her. "Whatever! Champagne was trying to keep her cool as she listened to Infinity run her mouth. Ace walked in the room to speak with Champagne. "The rest of you ladies can find something to do, Champagne we need to talk." Everyone walked out of the room, Champagne didn't know what was going to happen, Ace didn't look like he was angry with her so she wasn't worried that he would hit her, he had never put his hands on her before. He never had a reason too. "What's going on with my man Divine? Ace asked as he poured himself a drink. "He's alright" Champagne answered as she smiled. "So what's going on with you? I see you are spending a lot of personal time on these visits with him and I'm trying to figure out why that is? Ace looked at Champagne waiting to hear her response. "I'm sorry I didn't think it would be a problem because you were cool with him and I like talking to him." Champagne thought Ace would agree but he didn't. "I have known D for a long time since he was a kid and I got a lot of love for him. Therefore, I am telling you right now you need to erase any little feelings you have for him and do your fucking job, be a hoe that's what you came here to do. so do it and do it right, I didn't force you into this you chose to be here but if you want out say the word and you can go! Champagne could not believe Ace was standing there yelling at her like that. "Well I guess the best time to speak would be now. I've been thinking about everything and I don't want to do this anymore, I never wanted to do this but I got caught up, and before you ask yes I am in love with Divine and if he will accept my past I'll be with him, so I guess that means I'm leaving! Ace could tell she was sincere about her feelings for Divine and wanting to change. "Wait, Champagne! I never did this before. But I'm going to start with you" Ace went into his safe and pulled out some money and gave it to Champagne the other girls listened angrily from the next room. "I'm going to give you this, because you are a good girl and you have been good to me, this should help you get on your feet a little. Now as far as Divine is concerned you, yourself have to work on that." Champagne hugged Ace than proceeded to get her things but Infinity wasn't going to let her leave that easily in her mind she felt once a hoe always a hoe and a hoe is never allowed to walk away from the game. "Where the fuck do you think you going hoe? "I'm done with this life so I'm leaving" Champagne turn away to walk out of the room. "Oh you, leaving bitch I don't think so" Infinity blocked Champagne from leaving. "Move Infinity" Champagne tried to walk past but Infinity was not budging. "Make me move hoe" before Champagne could do anything Infinity pushed her down and started kicking her. "You thought you was going to walk out of here without getting your ass kicked" Champagne got up and started fighting back, then Ace ran in the room yelling. "Infinity back the fuck off, let her go" Infinity could not believe Ace was defending Champagne after what she had done. "How you just letting her walk out of here like that? Ace grabbed Infinity by her arm, "I said let her go" Champagne walked out of the house as the other girls stared and shook their head. Once she was gone, Ace told everyone to listen up and listen closely. "I let her go for my own reasons and last time I checked I didn't have to explain myself to anyone, if any hoe in here has a problem with that speak the hell up if not keep it moving, Infinity do that shit again and I'm going to beat your ass." No one said a word, not even Infinity. Everyone in that house was there because they wanted to be and no one wanted to go through the process of finding another pimp so everyone did as Ace said and kept it moving. The next day Ace went to see Divine so that he could speak to him. "What's up d? Ace sat down at the table, Divine wasn't expecting to see Ace but it felt good to see him. "What's up Ace" Ace peeped the look on Divine's face as he sat down. "You act like you're shocked to see me." "No I just thought it would be Champagne that's all, what's up with her? Champagne hadn't wrote him or been up to see him in a few days. "Well I came to speak to you about that, she left, she didn't want to be a part of the game anymore" Divine looked at Ace like he was crazy. "You joking right? Ace wasn't smiling at all. "I'm serious man, that girl is in love with you." "Damn" Divine thought to himself as Ace continued. "Man this game isn't for everybody; it can make a hoe or break a hoe. I knew from day one, that she had no business on those streets. She was better than that shit but I let her taste that life, I can't complain she always brought more money than problems to daddy.

115

Well enough of that shit, what's up with this lawyer you got, I hope he's doing his job right" Ace wasn't let Champagne's leaving bother him, he was more worried about Divine beating his case. "He will, I have trust in him" Divine knew he had to think positive. "Any info, on our lil friend Quan? Ace wanted Quan dealt with as much as Divine did. "I found out a few things from some clown ass niggas in here and I'm just waiting on some more info" the visit was almost over and Ace stood up to get ready to go. "Well look man I'm going to get on back to the real world you just maintain and focus on getting out of here." Divine headed back to his cell, he couldn't believe that Champagne left the hoe shit alone, to be with him and that Ace was cool with it. The weeks went by fast. Jeremiah was working overtime on the case. He wanted Divine to walk away with a clean slate and not have to serve any real time. He knew Divine was innocent he just had to prove it. Jeremiah knew Stephanie would be worse than a pit bull in the courtroom. He knew he had to walk in there with his head high and a lot of luck. Jeremiah was on his way out of the courtroom and bumped into Judge Dobbs, who decided to invite him to lunch. Jeremiah knew that it wasn't a friendly invite he most likely was going to get an earful about his choice in defending the case. . "Jeremiah, I hear you are representing a case that will be heard in my court room" Judge Dobbs didn't sound too pleased. "Yes I am sir" Jeremiah knew the conversation was about to get worst. "Well I don't know why you would involve yourself in something like that anyway" Jeremiah looked at Judge Dobbs with a confident grin "I believe that all clients are innocent until proven guilty." Judge Dobbs believed strongly Divine was guilty "you can't possibly think that clown is innocent!

"Actually I do sir" Jeremiah replied with a smile. "Well the word around town is that he's guilty" Before Jeremiah could respond he noticed the Judges attention was across the room, "I would love to have a taste of that! Jeremiah looked as the Judge's attention was focused across the room at two black females. Sir, you were saying? "Pardon me Jeremiah I was just enjoying the view" Jeremiah could not believe what he was hearing, Judge Palmer Dobbs liked black women. Jeremiah was shocked because he thought he was a racist, so he decided to try to get the Judge to confirm his speculations. "Enjoying what view" Judge Dobbs began to speak about what caught his attention. "Just look at them two black women over there, they are beautiful. Do not get me wrong I love my wife but those type of women do something to me. you mean to tell me you don't like what you see, oops I forgot your soon to be my son in law well if you wasn't dating my little girl I would tell you to taste some chocolate" Judge Dobbs was doing everything except drooling. "Excuse me sir" Jeremiah could not believe what the Judge was sitting there saying to him. "Jeremiah, stop acting like you don't know what I'm talking about." "Bingo" Jeremiah thought to himself, he finally had something on the Judge. Little did Jeremiah know some years ago before Amanda was born Judge Dobbs was having an affair with a housekeeper in his home and would have continued had his wife not have suspected anything and had her replaced. Mrs. Dobbs just didn't like the way her husband would look at her. "Well I have some errands to run so I'm going to cut this lunch short" Jeremiah wasn't sure if Amanda knew about her father and his love for black women, so he decided to keep it to himself. Jeremiah decided to visit Divine, to tell him about what he had discovered. "Hello Divine, how's everything going? Jeremiah sat down at the table with a grin on his face. "I'm still in here, so things must not be that great; man what's up with this case any new information? I know you got something and my trial is coming up" Divine kept hoping to hear that all charges were dropped but every black man know you are guilty until proven innocent. Jeremiah could tell that Divine was getting stressed. "look Divine I know I can beat this, but you have to work with me, I'm going to get you out of here, I just defended you to my girlfriend's father who swears up and down your guilty" Divine shook his head, "damn so even he thinks I'm guilty huh? Divine was trying his hardest to keep positive thoughts. "He sure does, at least that's what was said at lunch before he focused his attention on other things" Jeremiah had Divine's full attention, "other things? Jeremiah looked around the room before he let Divine in on the Judges secret. "It's a long story, put it like this the Judge really likes chocolate, you know what kind of chocolate, I'm talking about" Divine sat up and smiled, it was as if a light bulb just turned on in his head. "Say word, the Judge got the fever? Jeremiah didn't even realize that he just provided Divine with some good news. "Where were you at having lunch? Divine asked so he could make a mental note of the address. "That little restaurant across the street from the courts" Jeremiah still didn't have a clue. Divine didn't even want to talk about his case anymore after hearing that information. He asked Jeremiah to have lunch a few more times with the Judge. Jeremiah dreaded the Judges Company, but he could tell by the look on Divine's face, that he was on to something. He agreed, grabbed his briefcase to head back to his office.

Divine went back to his cell to work on the plan he had in mind for the Judge. He knew that he had to get a letter out to Ace to have some females at that restaurant. Divine grabbed his pen and pad and sent Ace a kite. "What up Ace, I need you to send a few honeys down by the courts to this restaurant. I need them to get at this Judge. His name is Judge Dobbs. Have one of them, go on the internet, and try to pull up a pic of him or something. Now is the time to get the bait out, One. " Divine mailed the letter out. He knew that Ace would put the girl's right on it. A week later Jeremiah decided to have lunch with the Judge. Ace had the girls stop by the restaurant a few times until they saw the Judge. On this particular day, they happened to walk in and sure enough, the Judge was there. Judge Dobbs watched as they walked by. They made sure to make enough eye contact with him to keep his attention. He wasn't even eating his lunch, he was too busy staring. One of them walked over and slipped him her number on a napkin. Judge Dobbs slipped the napkin in his pocket. Jeremiah knew that Divine had something to do with it. He wasn't going to let the Judge know what was going on. "Did she just slip you her number? Jeremiah asked pretending not to know what was going on. "She sure did and I will be giving her a call" the Judge licked his lips and he glanced to the table where the females were sitting. "Jeremiah thank you for lunch, I need to make a few calls, so we're going to have to wrap this up" The Judge left the restaurant in a hurry. Jeremiah left the restaurant laughing to his self because the Judge took the bait too easily. Judge Dobbs walked to his car, called the number on the napkin; he was greeted by a sexy voice "hello, is this the young woman who wrote her number on a napkin?

The voice on the other in replied. "Yes it is sweetie" Judge Dobbs was excited as hell. "Look when I can see you so we can spend some time alone? "Well, what do you have in mind? The voice on the other end replied. "A whole lot if giving the opportunity," Judge Dobbs was ready to have some fun. "Let me go get a room and I'll call you back with the information" the female on the other end hung up the phone" Judge Dobbs waited for the young lady from the restaurant to call him back with the hotel information. Infinity and Exstacy headed to get a hotel room and called Ace to let him know they had a date with the Judge.

"Hey, daddy! we bout to go on our little date with the Judge." Ace was happy to hear that. "Damn he moves fast doesn't he, make sure you girls blow his mind, call me when you get there I'll send a camera." Infinity hung up and her and exstacy went and got their hotel room. She called the Judge, gave him the address, and told him to head over in an hour. The girls waited for Ace to send someone with the video camera while Judge Dobbs got ready to meet them at the hotel. Infinity and Exstacy changed into their lingerie and waited for the Judge to arrive, Judge Dobbs arrived with some strawberries and the finest wine he could find. Exstacy waited until the Judge was drunk enough to the point he wouldn't notice her setting up the camera. As the night went on things were starting to heat up in the room with the Judge and the girls. Little did Judge Dobbs know everything he was doing, was being recorded. After they were finished, they slipped out of the room while the Judge lay passed out on the bed. They headed back to Ace to let him view the tape, Ace could not believe what he was watching. "Damn girls y'all really put it on him. I'm sure D will be happy to hear about this, I want you ladies to get another date with the Judge soon, and then I think we'll have his ass right where we want him." a few weeks passed and the girls met the Judge again for another kinky episode. "So what do you do exactly? Infinity asked as she climbed on top of the Judges lap. "I'm a Judge" Exstacy walked over to the Judge and rubbed the top of his head. "So you're a legal eagle huh, how about you show us your chambers" Infinity and Exstacy already knew who Judge Dobbs were but they weren't going to let him know that. "Maybe I will, can you girls come to the courthouse tomorrow, in between cases we can have a little fun" Judge Dobbs was enjoying himself as infinity and Exstacy worked their magic, they had him right where they wanted him. Two hours had passed and Judge Dobbs had to go to a meeting, he promised to make another date very soon. Infinity and Exstacy headed back to the house, to let Ace know that the Judge was planning to sneak them into his chambers tomorrow. Ace was impressed. "Oh he really taking a chance having y'all up in there, make sure you girls Dress to impress, keep it classy and give it to him straight no chaser." The next day the girls met up with the Judge in his chambers and had a little fun. A few days had passed and Ace went up to visit Divine to let him know how everything was going with the plan. "What's good D? Divine could tell by Ace's facial expression, he had good news. "What's up Ace? Divine sat down at the table and was ready to hear what Ace had to share. "I came to give you some good news; the girls did that thing you needed them to do, so whenever you ready to put that Judge business out there let me know." Divine was pleased with the news. "Give the ladies my thanks and tell them I'll be ready to handle that real soon." Divine told Ace that Keisha hadn't been up to see him in a while,

He knew that she was feeling some kind of way from their last visit. There was still no word on Quan but Ace let Divine know that he had the word out and as soon as he knew something, he would let him know. The visit was over and Divine had some moves to make. Ace headed back home to check on his girls. Divine decided to go to rec, hoping he would bump into the guys from Philly. After sitting around for a while he noticed them walking in. Divine waited a few minutes then walked to them to get some more scoop on Raymond. "Philly Philly what up! any more word on your people? Divine was hoping they had some news. "Who, that nigga Raymond? as a matter a fact my baby moms wrote me and told me her mom was sick and it wasn't looking too good. So I know she got in touch with him and most likely he'll be in Philly soon." That was exactly what Divine wanted to hear. "Oh is that right? Divine thought to himself. He wasn't sure if he could let them know why he really wanted to know where Raymond was.

****

Word got to Raymond down south, that his mother was sick. So he was making plans to head back to Philly. He let Quan know what was going and that he needed to go to check on his mother. Quan was ready to go anyway, he wanted to ride through the hood and see if he could get any information on Divine. Little did he know Divine had a few folks on the watch for him. Raymond and Quan got on the road early in the morning; their first stop was New York. Divine sat in his cell just waiting for word from Jeremiah because he trial date was coming up real soon; Divine wanted everything to fall into place before he went to court.

A few weeks later Jeremiah visited Divine to let him know he had two weeks left until his trial. Divine figured it was time for the girls to get at the Judge. Later on that day, he received a letter from Ace letting him know that Quan was seen in the hood, on more than one occasion. Divine knew he had to get Quan dealt with. The next day Divine called up Ace and told him, he needed a visit. Ace knew exactly what the visit would be about by the tone of Divine's voice. So he headed up to the prison. "What's up D? Ace knew that Divine had something on his mind. "I want that nigga Quan dealt with and dealt with quickly" Divine was pissed that Quan was really walking the streets as if shit was sweet. "I'll get on that soon" Ace was working on a very nice set up for Quan. Divine told Ace to let the girls get at the Judge; He wanted the Judge to get his before the court date. Once that was done, he wanted Ace to put the girls on the hunt for Quan, since his weakness was women Divine knew he could get him caught up. Ace knew what was on Divine's mind and he knew that the girls would be able to get the job done very well. He headed back to the apartment to give them the orders. Infinity and Exstacy contacted Judge Dobbs, to see if he would be up for some entertainment and sure enough, he was. Once they got him alone, they let him know what they wanted him to do and why he needed to do it. "Look all of this has been fun but now it's time to get down to business," Infinity said as she stood by the door. "What exactly are you talking about? Judge Dobbs looked a little confused. "You are the Judge in the Divine Williams case right? Exstacy walked up to the judge and asked.

"Yes I am why do you care? Judge Dobbs asked in a firm tone. "Don't worry about that, you need to make sure that he walks." Infinity said with a smirk. "Walks are you shitting me! That boy is guilty!" Judge Dobbs began laughing hysterically. "Well if he doesn't walk, you'll never hear another case again" infinity pulled out a vhs tape waving it back and forth. "You ladies can't do this I'm a Judge, besides that case will be heard by a jury and they will make the final decision" Exstacy walked over to the Judge and grabbed him by his collar. "Well Judge, you need to make sure that jury makes the right decision or we might just have to let everyone know how you like to get down, spankings and all." Judge Dobbs pushed her back "I didn't do anything but show you ladies a good time" Infinity started laughing "that's where you are wrong, you had a good time with two prostitutes, I wonder how your wife is going to feel about the video's we made." The Judge looked clueless "what, wait a minute you girls are prostitutes? Exstacy and Infinity laughed at the Judge's question, and Infinity replied. "Man you didn't think we really liked your ass did you? Now if you do what we asked you to do, we'll bury you're little secret" Infinity pointed to the vhs tape. Judge Dobbs was furious. "This isn't right; you can't do this to me! This is blackmail." "Actually baby we call it p. o. p" Exstacy giggled, she could tell the Judge didn't know what the hell they were talking about. " P.o.P! What is that? Infinity whispered in the Judges ear. "Power of pussy, maybe we should just bring the video to court, I'm sure everyone would love to see it." Judge couldn't let that happen, he tried to grab the tape from Infinity. "No, no, no there's no need, I'll do it just promise me none of this will get out. I'll do my best to make sure the jury makes the right call but that will be the first in history." Infinity kissed the Judge on the forehead. "well I guess it's a first time for everything." The girls left the hotel.

The Judge sat in the room in shock. He could not believe his career of 44 years was in jeopardy. Once back at the house, Infinity and Exstacy let Ace know the Judge was ready to play ball. Ace was pleased; he knew that the trial would go smooth for Divine. Now it was time to get Quan out of the way. A few days had passed and Infinity and Exstacy were on the hunt, they worked the area hoping to see Quan and after a few nights of coming up with nothing they finally spotted him or at least they hoped it would be him. They decided to walk over towards him to get his attention. As they crossed the street, Quan and Raymond noticed them. "Damn" Quan made sure they heard him. "Hello, how y'all doing? What y'all getting into tonight? Raymond's eyes were lit up like a Christmas tree. Infinity smiled and replied, "We're just hanging out." Quan walked over to Infinity and introduced himself and Raymond. "I'm Infinity and this is my home girl Exstacy" Quan like their names as well as their looks. "So I'm saying let's go somewhere and chill" Infinity agreed, her and Exstacy hopped into the car with Quan and Raymond. They knew they had to let Ace know what was about to go down but they didn't want Quan to know what was up. Raymond pulled up to a hotel; Quan went to pay for the room. "Yo cuz, run to the store right quick so we can get right, get me a nice size bottle" Raymond drove down the street to store. Infinity and Exstacy rode with him; they waited til he got out of the car to call Ace. "What up Daddy, you not going to believe this but we found that nigga Quan" Ace stopped what he was doing completely. "You sure it's him? "The nigga told us his name, and he's with a nigga named Raymond," Infinity told Ace that Quan wasn't driving the green car and that they were going to a hotel with him.

Ace told Infinity to make sure they get the job done right and then get out of the room as quickly as possible. As soon as Infinity hung up her phone, Raymond was walking back to the car. "Damn what you do go grocery shopping? Raymond put the bags in the car. "you funny shorty, I just had to make sure I had everything so I don't have to go back to the store." once back at the hotel Quan signaled Raymond to park the car, Infinity was hoping Quan had got separate rooms, but he didn't so they knew they had to work their plan out a little different. Once in the room the girls knew they couldn't get too drunk; this was a business call far from personal. Infinity decided to make her way to the bathroom to freshen up and Exstacy followed. Quan didn't know why they were going to the bathroom at the same time. "Damn y'all going to the bathroom together, what's up with that? Exstacy turned around and smiled. "We do everything together." Quan grabbed his crotch as he stared at Infinity's ass. "I hear that can I come? Infinity licked her lips and looked at Quan. "You will in a minute." once in the bathroom Infinity and Exstacy knew they couldn't talk to loud, they quietly spoke on their plan. "What the fuck are we going to do? "Be cool I'm going to get the nigga in the bathroom and then you handle the other one out there" Exstacy was nervous. "I hope we can do this shit" Infinity wanted Quan, she sent Exstacy to handle Raymond. Exstacy walked out of the bathroom she let Quan know Infinity was waiting for him. Infinity was ready; she always kept a surprise tucked away. Quan walked in the bathroom ready to get right. "Damn girl, what we bout to do take a shower? Infinity put her hand inside of his boxers. "No I just wanted a little alone time with you" "I hear that hot shit" Quan was hard as a rock. " why don't you sit right here so I can show you some things." Quan sat back on the toilet as Infinity worked him into her mouth. He was so blown, from the blowjob he was getting; he didn't see the razor blade she had inside her bag on the back of the toilet seat. a few moments later she climbed on top of him and began to ride him. Quan was enjoying every minute of it, while Infinity was waiting for the right moment to get at him. As soon as she knew, he was caught up in the moment she reached into her bag, pulled out her razor, and slit his throat. Quan didn't even see it coming, Infinity hopped up off of his lap and watched as he sat there bleeding. She whispered in his ear, "This one is for Divine mother fucker! Exstacy was taking her sweet time to handle Raymond. Infinity was mad as hell when she peaked out of the door and saw that Raymond was still alive. When she walked out of the room, Raymond didn't even notice her because his back was turned and he was too busy grinding. Before she could let Exstacy know she was finished, Raymond turned around. "Yo why the fuck, do you have blood all over you? Where the fuck is my cousin? Raymond hopped off the bed, before he could make it to the bathroom Exstacy hit him in his head with the lamp in the room and he fell out. "Bitch is you crazy, you out here fucking up a storm and I'm in there doing what we came here to do" Infinity grabbed Exstacy by her hair. "I'm sorry but the! Exstacy couldn't even finish "but the what? The dick had you caught up. Look, handle that nigga while I clean myself up right quick and we need to clean this room before we go." Exstacy pulled out her knife, and started stabbing Raymond up as Infinity cleaned herself up. Infinity was finished they used some soapy rags to wipe down the room. Once they were finished they left the hotel and headed back to the house to let Ace know the job was done. As soon as they walked in Ace was sitting on the couch ready to hear the news. "Are you sure that nigga is dead? Infinity sat down next to Ace. "He wasn't breathing when I left the hotel" Exstacy was very quiet, she had never killed anyone before, so she was a little shaken up. "What about the other one? Ace wanted to make sure everything was done correctly. "Exstacy handled him, she stabbed him up well" Infinity was too busy cleaning up to make sure Raymond was dead. Exstacy told Ace that Raymond wasn't breathing when she walked out the room, she never checked Raymond's body, in the back of her mind she hoped that he was dead. Ace walked over to his safe, pulled out two stacks a piece, and handed them to Infinity and Exstacy. "Well you girls need to lay low, as a matter of fact I think you girls earned a vacation, so why don't you get some things together and go down to Miami and enjoy yourselves but not too much, I need y'all back in a few days." Infinity and Exstacy packed up and headed down to Miami, to enjoy themselves and clear their heads. Ace went to visit Divine to let him know everything was taking care of. "What's going on D, I came to let you know that problem you had has been solved. "Ace was grinning ear to ear as he sat down to the table. Divine was pleased to hear that Quan was no longer an issue. "That's cool, my trial will be starting soon, how's everything else looking? "Well my girls took a little vacation but that other problem will be solved when they get back" Divine appreciated everything Ace had the girls do to help him. "When this is all over with we need to have a celebration" Ace agreed, it was almost over; Divine was about to be a free man. That night, Quan's body was found in the hotel, there was no sign of Raymond.

It was a day before the trial and Divine hoped that Judge Dobbs would stick to the script and not get a change of heart. In the event that he did Infinity and Exstacy, had that covered so they weren't worried about it. t Divine sat in his cell reading old letters that Keisha wrote him, after their last visit Keisha decided to keep her distance, she hadn't even wrote him. He wanted to see Keisha but not on a jail visit, He had been thinking about her a lot lately and was starting to feel something for her. He just wasn't sure what that was. He decided to drop a few lines to let her know he was thinking about her, and that he would see her soon. Jeremiah was ready for the trial to begin and he worked hard to prepare his argument for his client's defense. The prosecutor kept offering a plea, but he knew Divine refused. He was sticking to his not guilty plea.

Let the trial begin chapter 8

As the courtroom began to fill Infinity and Exstacy hurried in to make sure everything would go as planned. As the deputies were bringing Divine in, he looked around to make sure everyone was in place. He was confident about walking out of there. "All rise for the honorable Judge Palmer Dobbs" Jeremiah was nervous as hell, but he was determined to win his case. Stephanie prepared her opening statement and was ready to stick it to Jeremiah. Judge Dobbs quickly glanced around the courtroom, to see if the two females who were blackmailing him were in the courtroom; sure enough, they were and they were giving him evil looks. As deliberations began, Jeremiah called his first witness who stated that he saw the young woman walk into the apartment hours before Divine arrived. His testimony alone was enough to get a not guilty verdict; but Stephanie's cross-examination highlighted the fact that Divine was a well-known drug dealer and was found in the apartment with the body, along with narcotics. A few hours had passed and detective Bryant had taken the stand, he spoke briefly about the evidence that he had retrieved in the murder of Charlene Jenkins and how the evidence did not point to Divine as the murderer. After hearing statements the Judge ordered a 15-minute recess, he knew that he had to do something quick and he needed to speak with the jury. He ordered one of the deputies to bring the members of the jury into his chambers. Stephanie did not understand why the Judge was requesting a meeting with the jury, it seemed very odd to her. Once inside his chambers the Judge made it perfectly clear to the jury that no matter what they heard in the courtroom; they must acquit

Mr. Williams. One juror questioned the Judge. "Your honor, excuse me for disagreeing but I'm sure I speak for everyone, when I say he is guilty, he might not be guilty of all of the charges but he is guilty of something." Judge Dobbs was getting very upset by the juror comments. "Look I didn't call you in here for a debate. I said to make sure this ass hole is acquitted and that's that! Judge Dobbs ordered everyone out of his chambers; he couldn't believe that he was setting a criminal free, but he also had to think about his career and he wasn't going to jeopardize that or his reputation. He walked back into the courtroom to hear the closing statements, Jeremiah stood up and spoke highly of his client; how he was a good man being railroaded by the system and ask the jury to enter a verdict of not guilty. Stephanie highly disagreed she wanted the jury to convict Divine Williams. After hearing the final arguments of both sides the jury presented their verdict, neither juror was happy with the decision they had been forced to make, but they knew they had to go along with the Judges request. "We the jury, find the defendant Divine Williams not guilty! Everyone in the courtroom, looked shock to hear the verdict, Stephanie was pissed off. "Your honor how is that possible, the defendant is guilty! How could this jury sit here after hearing everything and say not guilty." Jeremiah looked on in disbelief he could not believe he had won the case. The smile on Jeremiah's face pushed Stephanie over the edge; she started yelling at the Judge in front of the jury. "you are hiding something, let me guess someone paid you off" "how dare you speak to me that way in my courtroom you are in contempt of court, deputy get misses Washington out of my court room, court is adjourned." Judge Dobbs slammed down his gavel and went back into his chambers. Divine turned around, looked at Infinity and Extasy, and winked his eye. Jeremiah began to wonder if he had anything to do with what just happened, "I'm not sure how this landed in our favor but it did" Divine shook Jeremiah's hand, "you did a good job J" The deputy's escorted Divine back to lock up as Jeremiah headed out of the court room. He was happy he had won the case but wasn't sure if it was all in his doing, he wanted to question Divine but he decided not to. "One up for me" he thought as he sat down on the courtroom steps to take everything in. As Jeremiah was getting up to walk down the block, he noticed the two females from the courtroom. He knew he had seen them somewhere before but he couldn't put his finger on it. One of them walked over to him and asked for the time. "No, way" Jeremiah thought to himself, they were the two females from the restaurant where he had lunch with the Judge. Did they have a connection with Divine and what were they doing in the courtroom? Why did Divine turn around and wink at them? Question filled Jeremiah's head as things began to seem very odd to him.

****

All the inmates in cellblock 5w72 stared in silence as inmate #032490 walked through the gate to enter the block. Watching him closely trying to read his facial expression, hoping he would speak on what happened at trial, but he quietly walked into his cell sat on his rack and began to write in his note pad. See he knew if he spoke on what happened, niggas would want to know every detail, so he kept quiet, ignoring the whispers of the other inmates. He began to put together everything in the cell that belonged to him but before he could finish getting his things, together one of the loudest niggas up in the block began to walk over to his cell. He noticed two deputies coming back to the block, as they approached the block they began to call out for him but they were interrupted. "Yo, What the fuck is going on?, this dude just walked in here like forty five minutes ago quiet as hell I know this nigga got a story to tell about his trial. And now y'all walking back up in here calling his number, what's up with that I know that nigga ain't going home, no way in hell the deputies yelled loudly "inmate # 032490, you ready to go it's time". He stood up grabbed his things and walked past the inmate who wanted to know so damn much and whispered "p.o.p nigga", as he entered through the gate he had a grin on his face that was indescribable, it was as if he was just giving the key to the city or some shit. No one knew that inmate # 032490 better known as Divine Williams played his cards right and that's why he was walking out of there and them niggas were still sitting in there, wondering how he beat the system. Divine grabbed his property and walked out of the prison gates, waiting for him outside to his surprise was Keisha. "Damn, I guess the good news traveled fast" Divine was happy as hell to see Keisha and she was looking good. "You know I wasn't going to let you leave here without a ride." Keisha smiled and got in the car. "I thought you wasn't fucking with me" Divine said as he leaned hit seat back. "After reading your letter and speaking to Ace I realized that I was wrong for trying to push you into something you won't ready for." Keisha drove Divine back to the city to meet up with Ace. As they pulled up, Divine leaned over and kissed Keisha. "What's that for? Keisha started blushing. "That's a little thank you kiss" Divine leaned over to kiss her again. "Thank You kiss for what?

Keisha knew the answer; she just wanted to hear him say it. "For you being there, being real with me and seeing something in me when the world saw something else" Keisha couldn't help but laugh. "Whatever, Don't try to get all mushy and shit because you free, I know what's really up with that kiss you trying to get some pussy ain't you? Divine laughed at Keisha so called prediction. "Damn, you said that like it's a problem" "Keisha was trying to play hard but divine saw right thru her. "I didn't say that you couldn't have any I was just speaking my mind." Divine look at Keisha knowing, that she wanted more than he was willing to give. "You know I'm trying to be wrapped up in no pussy permanently, I'm going to go in here, chat with my man Ace I'll be over there in a few hours to chill with you." Divine got out of the car, and headed inside to see Ace. "Alright" Keisha drove off to her house, to get ready for her night with Divine. Ace welcomed Divine with a big ass bottle of the finest and a few ladies. "You think you can handle this? Divine looked around the room very impressed by what he saw. "Can I handle it? Hell yeah" Ace laughed. "I almost forgot my girl Keisha got your head spinning! So what's up what's your game plan? Divine sat back on the couch scratching his head. "Well right now, I'm going to parlay maybe take a little vacation. Then when I get back I'm going to get with my connects, if they still willing to do businesses with a nigga and pick up where I left off." Ace smiled and agreed. "Well let me know when you ready and I'll do what I can from my end" Divine sat up with a smirk on his face. "Now that I know that nigga Quan is no longer a problem, I'm good." Ace put his glass down. "Well I'm not exactly sure if the problem was completely solved." Divine paused. "What do you mean by that? Ace

134

pulled Divine to the side. "Well, there was only one body found in that room and it was Quan's." Divine sat silently as he wondered where the fuck Raymond was at, Infinity and Exstacy listened as Ace filled Divine in on what happened that night at the hotel. Infinity was angry that Exstacy didn't get the job done. Now they had to look over their shoulder every time they are out in the street. Divine called Keisha and told her to pick him up. When Keisha arrived, Divine told her he wanted to take a vacation and he wanted her to go with him. "So what's up you going to leave with me? Keisha smiled. "I guess so" Keisha was happy that Divine invited her out of town; she knew it was the start of something new. "Before we roll out, I need to stop by my crib." While Divine was locked up Ace made sure the apartment was in good shape until he returned. Divine wasn't worried about anything being stolen or messed up; other than what the cops did the night of his arrest. "You sure you want to do that? Keisha asked on the way to Divine's crib. she knew that it was going to upset him. "I need to get my things out of there so I got just do it! As Keisha pulled up in front of the building, Divine prepared himself to go in, he hadn't seen the block since the night he got locked up, a lot of memories of that night flashed in his head as he unlocked the door. A teardrop rolled down his face as he walked past Jb's door. His boy was gone and it was nothing he could do. The cops did a good job of tearing up the place and making it obvious a crime was committed there. Divine grabbed some of his things and placed them in the living room, he walked into Jb's room to grab the pictures of them off his wall. As he walked past the bed, he noticed a box on the floor with more pictures in it, when he picked the box up he noticed an unopened envelope addressed to Jb. Divine opened the envelope; it was a letter from Jb's grandmother.

Dear Jb,

Before I go home to be with my lord, I wanted you to know some things, even though you have never asked me I feel it is my place to tell you about your father since I know that your mother is not going to step up and tell you who he is. When your mother was 16 she started messing around with an older man against my wishes and that's how she got pregnant with you, she wanted to give you up for adoption but I told her she had to face responsibilities, of course the weight was too much to bare. I had her send you to me and I raised you as my own. i would see your father a few times in the neighborhood when you were younger but I never let him know who you were and he never knew you existed,

A few friends told me that he was a pimp and I could not have you around that, but now that you are getting older if you want to meet him his name is Ace and he doesn't live too far from here. Now I am not sure if you will use this information or not but I could not have that on my conscience. No matter what happens, I want you to take care of yourself and stay true to your friends. I love you grandson.

Love always your grandmother"

Divine folded up the letter, put it in his pocket, and headed out of the apartment. He couldn't believe what he had just read. He now knew that Ace was Jb's father; it was too much of a coincidence.

Divine drove back to Ace's house to let him know what he just found out. "He is not going to believe this," Divine said shaking his head in disbelief. "Believe what? Keisha asked, wondering what Divine was talking about. "Looks like our man Ace was Jb's father." Divine headed into the house to give Ace the letter. "Read this" Ace unfolded the letter and began to read it as Divine looked on, Ace could not believe what he was reading he slammed the letter on the table. "Is this some kind of fucking joke? Divine knew Ace didn't believe the letter. "Man that's as real as it gets." Ace started banging his fist on the table while shouting. "You trying to tell me that the Charlene that I knew had a child, which was my son. And is the same child that is now dead." Ace put his head down and screamed out in anger. He couldn't believe that he had a son, but most of all he couldn't believe that he never got the chance to know him. "Look man I didn't mean to bring you down with the fucked up news I just thought you should know" Ace hugged Divine and thanked him for bringing the letter. "No, no, no you did the right thing and we did the right thing getting rid of that mother fucker Quan! "I'm going to bounce I'll call you in the morning before we roll out" Divine gave Ace a pound and walked out of the apartment. "Alright man you two be safe" Divine and Keisha went to her place. Keisha did her best to avoid talking about Jb. she knew he was on Divine's mind. "Are you ok? Keisha asked as she rubbed Divine's back. "I'm fine" Divine sat back in the chair trying not to dwell too hard. "You sure cause if you want to talk I'm here to listen" "no I'm cool I'm going to just relax and get ready for our trip" Keisha went into the kitchen and poured her and Divine some drinks. Divine wanted to take a shower, Keisha showed him where the towels were and went in her room to straightening up. Divine got out of the shower, walked into the room and stood in the doorway looking at Keisha. "Why you standing there like that? Keisha started giggling. "Like what, like this? Divine dropped the towel in the doorway and walked over to Keisha standing by the bed. He kissed her on the back of her neck and began to take off her clothes; Keisha laid back on the bed as Divine worked his tongue up and down her body and slowly placing it between her thighs, she moaned as Divine licked passionately inside of her. Divine climbed on top of her and they made love most of the night, Keisha fell asleep in Divine's arms. The next morning Keisha was up making Divine a nice size breakfast. Divine woke up and walked into the kitchen. "Let me find out you can cook" Keisha smiled. "Yes I can" Divine wrapped his hands around her and kissed her on her neck. "It smells good" filled with excitement Keisha asked "what time are we leaving? Divine pointed to the food, grinned and said "Right after this" Divine and Keisha packed everything up after breakfast and headed to the airport. "So where are we going? Keisha asked as they pulled into the airport parking lot. "I thought we go down to Miami" Divine was spontaneous in making his decision. He wanted to go where the weather was good and the mood was right. Once they arrived in Miami, they checked into a very nice hotel and rented a car to go see the sights. Keisha was happy to be with Divine, she was hoping he felt the same. Divine made her feel like a queen, shopping sprees fancy dining hot nights on the town. After a few weeks of fun in the sun, they headed back to NYC.

Months had passed and Divine was close to being back on top of his game, Keisha was starting to feel neglected, she didn't like the fact that he was spending so much time with Ace. One night she decided to go to Ace's house to see what Divine was doing; when she walked in Ace was on the couch sleep next to one of the girls and looked as if he had been up all night getting twisted. There were empty liquor bottles everywhere. Keisha made her way to the back room, as she walked down the hall she heard music along with moaning the closer she got to the door she noticed the door was cracked. Unprepared for what she was about to see, she decided to take a peak. Her heart dropped as she looked into the room she saw Divine having sex with Infinity and Exstacy. Tears filled her eyes as she watched Divine sex Infinity. As bad, as she wanted to walk in the room she turned around and walked quietly out of the house. Two days had passed since she had saw or spoke to Divine, how could he do this to her she thought as she cried over and over to herself, the phone had rung and it was Divine. Having no clue that Keisha saw him he spoke on the phone as if nothing was wrong. "Hey baby what you doing? He asked in a laid-back tone. Keisha was trying to keep her cool as she responded to him. "I'm laying down what are you doing? Divine answered, still clueless that he was busted. "I'm on my way in the house; you know I had business out of town." Keisha replied sarcastically "whatever D" and hung up the phone. Divine didn't know what to make of her hanging up on him but he could tell she had an attitude. He pulled up to the house, grabbed his bags and walked in, Keisha was sitting on the couch with her face frowned up. Divine laid his keys on the table and asked Keisha, "Why the fuck did you hang up on me? Keisha already knew that question was coming but she felt he didn't have the right to question her because he was in the wrong. She stood up and replied in a loud tone. "Don't come in here questioning me about what I did" Divine looked confused as he asked her "what the hell is your attitude about? Pissed that he was standing in her face playing dumb she started flipping. "Nigga do I look stupid to you, I saw your ass fucking those bitches and you going to stand here and play stupid get the fuck out" she said grabbing his keys and slinging them across the room. Still thrown off by Keisha's rampage and unsure exactly what bitches she saw him fucking he kept his cool and asked with a grin. "You saw me fucking what bitches? Keisha looked at him as if she wanted to pick up something and knock his ass out wondering why he wouldn't just come clean she said, "oh my lord you really trying to play me like I'm stupid nigga! Infinity and Exstacy; that's who." Divine sat down on the couch speechless he didn't know that Keisha had saw him or how she got into the crib. "You don't have shit to say now do you, I bet your ass didn't think I still had keys to that damn house" Divine tried to calm the situation down. "Keisha let me explain" Keisha was in full bitch mode. "Explain what? You can't explain shit to me" before Keisha could say anything else she ran to the bathroom barely making it, throwing up all over the toilet seat. "Are you ok? He asked as he stood in the bathroom door. Keisha grabbed a towel and wiped her mouth. "Leave me alone D! Divine walked over to Keisha and stood by the sink. "What the hell you mean leave you alone? I'm just asking you if you are ok? Keisha ignored Divine as he continued to ask her if she was alright, she rinsed out her mouth and walked into her bedroom. Divine followed her trying to talk to her, but she wasn't trying to listen. He tried kissing her but she pushed him away. Divine grabbed some clothes and went to take a shower. Keisha grabbed her keys and drove to the clinic to get a pregnancy test. She knew she had been a little late but now she was vomiting. Sitting in the clinics so many thoughts flowed through Keisha's mind. She was pissed off at Divine and the thought of her being pregnant wasn't sitting too well with her. She was examine, then waited for her results. After sitting there for a half an hour, she found out, she was indeed pregnant. The tears rolled down Keisha's face as the doctor read her results. She walked out the clinic, crying and confused, she wasn't ready for a baby at all. Once she got home she noticed Divine on the couch sleep, she walked past him and went into her room to lie down. There was no way she was going to tell him she was pregnant, and it was no way she was going to have his baby. A few hours later Keisha woke up and Divine was gone. She wondered if he had went back to Ace's so she got Dressed and went over there, when she walked in she didn't see Divine or Ace. Infinity was sitting on the couch and wasn't pleased when Keisha walked in. "Ace isn't here so what do you want? Keisha looked down the hallway towards the back room. "Is Divine here? Infinity got up from the couch and walked up to Keisha putting her hands in her face. "Do you see him here? Keisha shoved Infinity back. "Look bitch; let me tell you something you better stay the fuck away from my man! Infinity busts out in laughter. "Your man, hoe please" Keisha rolled her eyes at Infinity. Who the fuck is you calling a hoe? Infinity replied sarcastically. "If the stiletto's fit than wear them, oh I forgot you tryna be a square ass bitch, I see why you want to fuck with him but I'm not sure why he wanna fuck you." Keisha and Infinity got into an intense argument. "Why you mad Keisha cause I fucked Divine; bitch don't hate this pussy hate ya man" Keisha gave a face laugh. "Whatever bitch! Their shouting match caused the other girls to run from the back, Keisha was tired of arguing with Infinity, and she grabbed her bag and headed home. As she was pulling up she noticed Divine parked in front of her house. Keisha got out of the car and started to walk into the house, Divine was right behind her.

" come here, Keisha let me talk to you." Keisha walked into her room. "Fuck you D, go be with that bitch Infinity" Keisha wasn't trying to hear anything he had to say. "Look I know you hurting behind that shit I did. all I can do is apologize, I was over there having a few drinks; chilling and one thing led to another." Divine was trying his best to be honest but it was not working. "What do you want me to say? It's ok that you fucked that bitch because you were drunk" Keisha sat on the bed and started crying. Divine tried to hug her and she pushed him away. "I don't know why I thought I could be with you anyway" Keisha got up off the bed and grabbed Divine's bag out of her closet. "So you want me to leave, over some pussy you don't own me bitch" Keisha walked over to Divine and slapped him in his face. Divine grabbed her and pushed her on the bed, he had never put his hands on a woman before, but he wasn't going to let Keisha just disrespect him. Keisha tried to lunge at Divine and he slammed her on the floor, knocking her bag down causing her papers from the clinic to fall out. Divine looked down and picked the papers up. "I guess that explains why the fuck you was in here throwing up, so you pregnant? Keisha got up from the floor and tried to snatch her papers from Divine. "Give me my shit." Divine would not give her the papers, "answer my question" Keisha looked at Divine with tears in her eyes and asked him. "What do the papers say? Keisha told him she wasn't having the baby so he didn't have to worry about it. Divine grabbed her and told her that he didn't want her to get an abortion, and apologized to her for fighting with her. Keisha walked over to the couch and started crying, she wasn't sure if Divine was ready for a child. He promised her that he would be there for her no matter what decision she made after a few hours of talking and getting Divine to promise he would stay away from Ace's apartment, she decided she would have the baby. A few months had passed and Keisha's belly was starting to grow and everything was going smooth between her and Divine, so far he was keeping his word and staying away from Ace's house. Whenever they needed to meet, he would have Ace come to their crib. Divine was back on top and planning to move Keisha and the baby out of the city after the baby was born. Everybody in the hood was happy to see Divine still doing his thing after all he had been through; he was still the nigga to go to for anything. He had made a few promises before he came home to put a few dudes on and he stuck to his word. Divine was rebuilding G.M.C one soldier at a time and he was prepared for anyone that felt they wanted to cross him.

The family thing Chapter 9

Keisha sat in her hospital room waiting for Divine to bring her some real food, she was happy her pregnancy was finally over; Divine Jr. came in the world weighing 8lbs and 9 oz and he resembled his father in every way. Divine made his son a promise that unlike his father he would never walk out on him. Keisha was ready to be discharged and head to her new home that Divine had purchased for them down in Florida. Keisha was more than ready for the move and Divine wanted to get her and his son out of New York.

****

Months had passed and Keisha was enjoying her new life in Florida. Divine was still making trips in and out of state, she didn't complain because the rewards were lovely. Divine promised to purchase her some property to get her salon up and running, after little Divine was old enough to start school. Keisha never questioned Divine she left all of her doubts and past issues in New York. Divine was starting to get tired of the hustling routine but he wasn't going to quit until he was financially equipped to do so. He kept his soldiers on their toes day to day hustle to hustle. Every now and then, he would creep with Infinity; it was something about her he couldn't leave alone, far from love more like lust. he made sure to keep his dealings with Infinity away from Keisha; it wasn't too hard to do because she was miles away. Divine was in love with Keisha but his love for her didn't keep him away from Infinity. The two of them were like night and day and Divine was having his cake and eating it too.

Divine pulled up to Ace's crib and waited for infinity to come outside, he needed her to ride with him to handle some business, the one thing Divine loved about her is she never told him no. Infinity walked to the car on her diva shit, weave down her back, smelling nice looking good. "So how's the family life treating you? She asked as she got in the car. Why are you worried about that? Divine knew she was trying to be funny with her question. "Damn I'm only asking a question" Infinity could careless how family life was for Divine; his little family didn't keep him away from her. "Well if you must know, it's good" Divine smiled. "Must not be too good, cause every chance you get you here with me" Infinity, knew she was right, but Divine didn't want to hear it. "look don't start the bullshit." "I'm not starting anything, that's you" "look I need you to do some things for me" "isn't that always the case, and what am I going to get out of it? Besides some dick what more do you want? Divine asked with a smirk. "Nigga please, I can get that from anywhere," Infinity said as she bragged about her clientele. "Damn, you want to go shopping? Divine threw a stack of fifty-dollar bills at Infinity. "For sure" Infinity smile and put the stack in her bag. Infinity knew she could work Divine into giving her everything except his heart she had always did what he had asked of her and therefore she felt he owed her so much. Divine dealt with Infinity for reasons other than sex, he knew he could get her to do anything; she was in love with him and down to get money, so he used that to his advantage. Infinity loved the fact that she was fucking Keisha's man; even a baby couldn't change that. She eagerly waited for the day to rub it all in Keisha's face. Divine needed Infinity to make some drug runs for him, since she was a female it would be easier for her to get away with it. whatever couldn't fit up in her, he would tape to her stomach. Divine purchased maternity clothing for Infinity so that she could look the part. Infinity hated when she had to play pregnant, she wasn't into the motherly thing. She thought she looked too good to be walking around with a big ass belly. Divine always had his ways to convince her to play the role. Divine was doing his thing and so far so good, problems were always kept to a minimum. He still wondered what ever happened to Raymond, he knew if they ever bumped heads, he would handle him quick. Divine spent the whole week up in New York; handling business and chilling with Infinity when everything was done he headed back home to Florida. On his way home, he called Keisha and told her that he wanted to go out to dinner later and to pick him up from the airport. Keisha got Dressed and waited a few hours before she drove to the airport. On the way to the restaurant Keisha noticed Divine was a little distant but she just figure he was worn out from the trip, Divine Jr. was getting bigger and looking more and more like his father. Keisha hoped every day that he wouldn't follow in Divine's footsteps. At dinner, Divine told Keisha that he was going to invite his mother down to stay for a few weeks; Denise had not seen her grandson since he was born and it would be nice to have his mother around. Divine was planning to be away longer than a week on his next trip to New York, Keisha wasn't happy about Divine's plans; she didn't understand why he had to turn right back around and go back to NY. Keisha gave Divine the silence treatment on the drive home. "What's wrong with you? Keisha was trying her best to keep her cool in the car but she couldn't. "I'm not understanding, why you have to leave and you just got back"

Divine wanted Keisha to understand that he was making moves for them but no matter what he said, she still was upset. "It's business and I need to go handle it." Keisha didn't want to hear that. "Why can't you get one of your soldiers to make this run? "Look them niggas are good but they ain't great and if I want shit to get done right I need to do it myself" Divine wasn't going to change his mind or his trip plans so Keisha changed the subject. "Well when is your mother getting here? "she'll be here tomorrow night and just so you know she's going to want to go shopping so I'll make sure I leave enough for the two of you to have some fun" Divine packed his bag for his trip and headed to bed. He had to be at the airport at eight in the morning and his cab would be at the house six in the morning. Things were really starting to bother Keisha. Divine was hardly around and as soon as they were able to spend time together, he had to turn right back around and leave. Divine jr. was getting older and Keisha felt like she was raising him by herself, even though her son never wanted for nothing Divine made sure of that but he was missing out on what really mattered having his father around. Denise waited at the airport for Keisha to pick her up; she was ready to have some out of town fun since she had never been out of New York. "Hey Keisha, how you doing? Keisha was happy to see Denise and have another adult around. "Hey Denise" Denise eyes lit up when she saw Divine jr. "look at my handsome grandson how's grandma's baby? Divine Jr. smiled as his grandmother picked him up and walked to the car. "So do you want to go straight to the house or go to eat? Well I ate on the way, so we could just go to the house" Keisha helped Denise put her bags in the car and they went to the house.

147

Denise wanted to see Divine and was a little upset that he wasn't there when she arrived. "So when will Divine be back? "Oh he'll be home in two weeks two weeks" that is a long time, are you cool with that? Keisha didn't want Denise to know Divine's absence was bothering her so she kept her cool. "It doesn't bother me." Denise could tell that something was bothering Keisha but she wasn't going to pry. When they pulled up to the house Denise was very impressed at the layout , once inside she got a tour of the house , Keisha put on some movies and they sat up for a few hours talking. The next morning Keisha took Denise to the mall to hang out and do some shopping.

****

Divine pulled up the Ace's around 4 pm, Infinity was already waiting for him outside but he needed to speak to Ace, when he walked in he noticed Ace acting a little odd. "What's up Ace you alright? "Yeah man I'm cool, just thinking over some things" Divine sat down on the couch; he could tell Ace had some things on his mind. "Like what? Ace sat down across from Divine, and put it all out there for him. "Man I'm getting too old for this shit, I'm ready to just put this all behind me" Divine laughed he didn't believe Ace at all. "Yeah, whatever you giving up the pimp game" Ace wasn't laughing at all. "shit, all my hoes are getting caught up in they own thing" Divine stood up and walked over to Ace "let me find out your pimp hand done turned soft." "Man I don't have time to be running behind no hoe, I'll just let this shit go" Divine looked down the hall and noticed none of the girls were around, not even Exstacy. Ace told him that she was strung out on the pipe and wasn't allowed back in the house. "Damn" Divine thought to himself.

Exstacy was Infinity's right hand girl, they were always together, but after that night in the hotel with Quan and Raymond she wasn't the same person. Ace walked over to the window and noticed Infinity sitting on Divine's car. "I'm shocked Infinity ass won't right behind her but she too busy choking on your dick to get strung out" Divine laughed aloud and said," man stop playing, it's not even like that." "Who you trying to fool D? I knew you two were getting down from day one. You know hoes like to talk, but that's on you. She's a good moneymaker but that bitch has ruthless tendencies and if it comes down to you or her what choice do you think she going to make? Divine wasn't trying to believe what Ace was telling him about Infinity. "Shit she cool she wouldn't play me" Ace laughed aloud. "Ok keep thinking with your little head instead of the big one." Divine walked outside to the car, he had errands to run and Infinity was right by his side. He told her Ace was giving up the pimp thing but he didn't tell her what Ace had said about her. After a few hours of driving, Divine decided to check into a hotel to rest. The next morning they continued their trip, once business was handled, Divine dropped Infinity off and headed back to the airport to make his way home. Infinity decided that since Ace no longer was doing the pimp thing that she would get money for herself even though she didn't have her right hand girl running with her anymore. Infinity worked the track solo. Exstacy was still on the track, she frequented the corners with hoes that were strung out on crack, cocaine, and heroin whatever knocked a bitch off her toes. Infinity got it in on the track; nothing was going to stop her from getting that money. She wasn't worried about any pimps trying to get at her because they knew who Ace was and they respected him.

Divine finally made it back home, when he got in everyone was sleep so he quietly took a shower and joined Keisha in bed. The next morning Keisha was up and happy to see that Divine had made it back home. Denise decided to stay a few more days; she was in no rush to return to NY. Divine had other plans for his mother he wanted to take her to look at some houses because he was planning to move her closer to him. Denise wasn't trying to leave NY, it was in her blood the only placed she had lived since birth. Divine didn't want his mother in New York for a lot of reasons mainly because he knew how the game was played and what happened to Charlene, he didn't want his mother to be in harm's way at all. Denise promised Divine she would think it over and get back to him with her decision but she still wanted to go sightseeing. They drove by a few neighborhoods close by to look at some houses; Divine hoped his mother would see something she liked so he could possibly get an answer before she went home. Out of the six houses, they went to look at only one really caught her attention. "Now this is somewhere I can live, this is nice, double driveway, swimming pool, nice front yard, double bath, four bedroom" Denise said as she admired the property.

"I don't think I need all those rooms" Divine looked at his mother and smiled. "Yeah you will, cause when your grand kids get out of hand they will be right over here" Denise looked at Divine like he was crazy.

"Excuse me grand kid I only have one" Divine laughed. "Who said I was finish? Denise decided to use the opportunity to say something to him about not being home as much. "Well the way you stay gone; don't look like you have time to make anymore." "You said that like I'm gone all the time! Denise decided to have a heart to heart with her son.

"Divine it's just you and I, right here right now so be honest with me, are you messing around on that girl when you gone? Because if you are, you need to let that girl move on and be happy" Divine never really sat down and had a grown up conversation with his mother, he damn sure wasn't going to tell her he was cheating on Keisha. "When I'm gone it's business that's all, Keisha isn't complaining." "Hell I wouldn't complain neither if I had a nice house and a nice car" Denise wasn't sure if Divine was understanding what she was trying to say. "So why are you telling me I should leave her? Divine his mother meant well but he really didn't want to hear it. "you missed the whole point I didn't say to leave her, I said if you are out there messing out around; to let her go on and be happy don't put her through the bullshit. Money is not everything and I hope you know that you can have all the money in the world and be miserable as hell," Denise shook her head, as she listened to Divine go on and on. "Well that's the mother of my child so I'm going to be with her" Divine wasn't trying to argue with his mother but he could tell she was getting upset. "Did you just hear yourself, you said the mother of your child; as if it's cute that you two are not married. Denise was speaking from her own experience with Divine's father and she didn't want him to make the same mistakes. "I thought we came out here to look at houses why you tripping ma? Divine, I'm not tripping I'm just trying to talk to you, I'm not trying to make you feel a certain way I'm not Judging you. I just want to that you do the right thing by Keisha and your son." Denise gave Divine a hug and they got back in the car to head back to his house. Divine and Denise pulled up to the house, the smell of the barbecue stopped them right in the driveway. Music was blasting, Keisha was cooking outside Divine Jr. was in his miniature pool having fun. "Something sure smells good back here" Denise complimented Keisha. Divine walked to the back to see what Keisha was making. What you got over there? Keisha opened up the grill with a smile. "Chicken, hamburgers, shrimp" Divine was ready to eat after hearing the menu. "Damn all of that? Keisha laughed and replied. "Yes all of that, it's some potato salad in the fridge." The food was done, plates were made and everything was all-good. Denise didn't want to stay up to late because she was flying out in the morning, so after eating and playing with Divine Jr. she headed to bed. The next day Denise was on her back to New York and Keisha had a few bones she wanted to pick with Divine. "Now that your mother is gone, you want to explain why the hell every time the phone rang and I answer it there is no one on the other end? "How do you know it's not the wrong number? "Wrong number my ass, funny it was happening until you got your ass in the house! "Look, I said it probably was the wrong damn number! Keisha knew better than to believe that, what Divine didn't know is on the night that him and Infinity stayed in the hotel, she took the number from his phone while he was in the shower, she knew it was his home number because the same number kept blowing up his phone. Keisha didn't know who it was because they wouldn't say anything but she sure as hell didn't think it was Infinity because she believed Divine when he told her he wouldn't mess with her anymore. Divine really thought it was someone just dialing the wrong number, Infinity didn't have his home number and she was only allowed to call his cell phone at certain times. Keisha changed the subject and accepted the fact that maybe Divine was really telling the truth, she didn't have any evidence that it was a female , so she just left it alone. A few months had passed and things with Keisha and Divine seemed to be getting better, he was spending less time on the road and more time at home with her and little Divine. He finally got her that shop she wanted even though Divine Jr. wasn't in school yet but they had found a nice babysitter for him until Denise moved down there. Keisha got accustomed to running her own shop. She hired some good hair stylists in the area and things were really starting to take off, with Keisha doing her thing at the shop Divine was able to do what he had to do without Keisha beefing with him. Divine decided it was time to take another road trip, so he picked Divine jr. up early from the sitter and dropped him off with Keisha at the salon. When he walked in, every female in the salon turned her head. Divine had never been in the shop so no one knew what he looked like, it was like throwing a piece a bread in central park and expecting the pigeons not to go crazy. Keisha watched as Divine became the focus of every one in there. Divine walked up to Keisha gave her a kiss and   told her he had to makes moves so he decided to get Divine jr. early. Keisha knew what that meant; he was going out of town. "So, when you coming back? Divine smiled and gave Keisha a hug and said, "I'll be back in a few weeks" Keisha wanted to say more but she was at work so she kept her thoughts to herself. As Divine walked out of the salon, one of the girls decided to be nosey. "How long you two been together? Keisha kept her response very short. "long enough" Keisha didn't say more than that and was hoping she wasn't asked anything else, she wasn't about to discuss her personal life with them even though she knew behind her back things were going to get said. Divine was on his way to NY but he wasn't going to scoop Infinity, he was taking care of business solo this time and he really wasn't in the mood for Infinity. As soon as she heard he was in NY she was blowing up his phone, finally after the sixth call he answered and told her he would call her back. Divine was trying to focus on business and he didn't need any distractions. Infinity did not appreciate Divine avoided her, especially when she felt he owed half of his success to her. When he needed something done, he was blowing up her phone and now he didn't want to be bothered. A few hours had passed, Infinity decided to call his phone again this time he decided to answer. "Let me find out you don't know me," Infinity said on the other end of the phone with an attitude.

"If I didn't know you than you wouldn't have my number," Divine replied sarcastically. "Whatever, come get me I'm bored." that's all Infinity wanted was to be up under Divine and he saw right through her. "What! it ain't no money on the track? Infinity laughed, "it's always money on the track but I'm trying to see you" he already knew that and he wanted to see her to. "Give me like a hour I'll be there to pick you up" Divine dropped his boys off and headed over to scoop Infinity, as always they went to a hotel to fuck most of the night. That's all she wanted and as long as she didn't start to catch feelings everything would be cool. Divine woke up the next morning and got himself ready to go to the airport and head back home, he called Keisha to check in, she was heading out the door on her way to a hair show in Georgia, that meant that he was coming home to an empty house. Divine just arriving at the airport and Infinity was blowing up his phone. "Didn't I just leave you? "Damn, you act like you don't miss me

I know you do, cause that bitch is not putting it down like me and we both know I taught her everything she knows" Infinity was filled with confidence as she bragged about her bedroom skills. "Is that right? Divine snickered. "You silly as hell! Keisha is not even home, she went out of town" Divine didn't even realize he just gave Infinity an indirect invite. "Ooh, I might just have to make a trip down there" that's all Infinity needed to hear, Divine was going home to an empty house.

"Chill that's ok; you need to stay in NY" "so you telling me if I leave on the next plane you wouldn't want to see me? Divine got real quiet on the other end of the phone. Infinity knew he wasn't going to say no. "Exactly! I'll call you when I land" Infinity hung up the phone, got her money together and was ready to hop on a plane to Florida. She didn't give a fuck about Keisha finding out. Divine couldn't believe Infinity was bold enough to bring her ass down there but he knew telling her no would only make her do it anyway. When he got home, he showered changed clothes and waited for her call. A few hours passed and Infinity was in Florida, Divine picked her up and took her to get something to eat, then they headed to his house. Infinity was amazed when she pulled up she couldn't believe how big the house was and if she wasn't already jealous of Keisha; then she would be. When she walked, the first thing that caught her eye was a large portrait of Keisha, him and Divine jr. Infinity couldn't deny that it was a big and beautiful house. "Damn" she thought to herself as she looked around. "That bitch got all of this for what? Pushing out a baby cause she don't do nothing else" Infinity After wasted no time speaking her mind. Divine poured some drinks, lit some candles to set the mood and change Infinity's attitude.

Later on that night, Divine and Infinity went upstairs to the bedroom; they had sex in every room except his son's room. Keisha had no knowledge at all that Divine was getting it on in their house. Infinity loved it and didn't feel bad at all, she was getting it on with Divine in a house that him and the bitch she couldn't stand shared. The next day Divine took Infinity shopping Miami style and she loved every minute of it, she wanted to get some clothes none of the other girls was rocking on the New York track. Whatever she wanted, she got no questions asked. Later on that night Keisha called Divine and told him she would be home in the morning, Divine knew that he had to get the house cleaned up and Infinity back to NY before Keisha arrived. Infinity wasn't ready to leave she was loving the money, sun, the sex, and everything else. "Looking like you need to get back to NY before she gets home" Divine wanted to get infinity out of there as soon as possible. "Fuck that I'm not ready to leave" Infinity didn't care that Keisha was on her way back, Divine wasn't trying to get caught up behind her being stubborn. "Stop playing with me" Divine grabbed Infinity by her arm to show her he wasn't joking. "Fuck it then I'll go but I'm coming back next weekend so you need to get a fly ass hotel room and make plans" Divine shook his head at Infinity's request. "You crazy with that one" Divine drove Infinity back to the house to pick up her things and quickly get her to the airport. He wasn't sweating what he had done, he just wanted to get the house cleaned up before Keisha got home. The next morning Keisha pulled up, when she walked in she was shocked to see Divine had went shopping and had cleaned up better than she did before she left. "Did you miss us? She asked as she walked over to Divine sitting on the couch.

"What do you think? Divine picked up Divine jr. "Did you have fun? "Yeah it was very nice down there, I had a good time" Keisha pulled her appointment book out to see if she had any appointments. "Did lil man act up? Divine asked as he put lil Divine down to play with his toys. "No he was good, you know he don't act up with me" Keisha smiled. "I don't think he act up with anybody, well what you have to do today? "I need to stop by the shop for a few minutes but I'm not working today, why what you have to do today? Divine replied. "Nothing I'm chilling, I don't have anywhere to go and nothing to do til next weekend" Keisha raised her eyebrow at him; she knew he was going to break out soon. "What's next weekend? "Business as usual" Divine wasn't planning on going too far, he just wanted to make sure he was able to get away when Infinity came back. The next day Keisha went to the shop, she picked up a few things, and headed back to the house with Divine and their son. They planned to have a family day out; at an amusement park, Divine hadn't heard from Infinity since she left. He knew he would hear from her soon. Infinity was up in New York hitting them hard on the tracks. The tricks loved her but the other hoes were hating on her hard. She was trying to get up enough money to get a nice little crib down there not too close to Divine but close enough. She didn't tell Divine her planned because she knew he would oppose but if she had her way it would be happening real soon. The weekend had rolled around and Infinity made her way back down to Florida. Divine met her at the airport and took her to a hotel close by the airport because he wasn't trying to be anywhere close by his house. Infinity wanted to go shopping but Divine told her she would have to wait. he didn't want to risk being seen around the city with her, and he didn't t trust her to go by herself. They spent the whole weekend, in the room; Infinity was pissed. She could not believe Divine would not let her go out. "Why are you acting like a pussy? Divine looked over at Infinity like she was crazy. "What the hell did you just say? "I said your acting like a pussy, scared of your baby mama trapped all up in a damn room." Infinity's bitching was annoying Divine. "First of all watch your mouth, and I'm not scared of anyone; it's about respect, how the fuck I look flaunting your ass around" Infinity laughed. "You'll look good, shit you talking about respect you wouldn't know respect if it bit you in your ass! Infinity started putting her clothes to ready to leave. "Look I promise, next time I'll take you shopping" Infinity walked into the bathroom with a serious attitude. "Oh next time you will be taking me shopping you better believe that! Divine drove Infinity to the airport and waited with her until her plane arrived. Once she boarded her plane, he headed home acting like he had been out of town all along. Keisha was sleep when Divine got in, so he showered and went to bed. The next morning Divine got up and headed in the kitchen, Keisha was on the phone. Divine could tell by her tone that she was upset with the person on the other end. "Yo who is that? Keisha slammed the phone down. "One of my girls from the shop" Keisha was highly upset as she grabbed her bag and keys to walk out the door. "What's up everything ok? "No, I have to get down there because someone is about to get fired" Divine knew that Keisha wasn't playing at all. "Oh damn" Keisha rushed out the door to head down to the shop to set somebody in order. Someone let the new girl who was only supposed to do shampoo, put a relaxer and she damaged the customer's hair. Once she arrived at the shop, she apologized to the customer and did her best to fix her hair. Keisha didn't fire the shampoo girl, but she made an announcement foe everyone in the shop to keep the mistakes to a minimum. Later on that night Keisha locked up the shop and headed home, Divine was sitting up with Divine Jr. playing the operation board game; Keisha was tired so she went straight to bed.

****

up in New York Infinity was doing her thing, she was working the track and the clubs Infinity was getting money nonstop, her plans to have enough money to buy a house were looking real good. Infinity decided when Divine came back up to New York she would finally tell him her plan. Divine was planning to head up to NY in a few weeks, he wanted to go and handle everything before Denise came down. She finally decided to move down and picked the house with the four bedrooms. Now that Divine knew his mother was moving closer to him he could really handle his NY business like he needed to. He knew if something went wrong, he wouldn't have to worry about his mother getting hurt. Denise decided shortly after returning home , that moving closer to her son would be a good idea. A few weeks went by and Denise was finally living in Florida. Keisha helped her decorate the house, Denise decided to decorate a room just for her grandson to sleep and play in when he came over. Every week Denise was right at the shop getting her hair done and out shopping on the weekend her and Keisha were becoming real close, Keisha felt a bond with Denise that she hadn't felt with her own mother. The last time Keisha saw or spoke to her mother was when she left Texas all those years ago. Keisha was hurting on the inside, she wanted to visit her mother but she knew her mother would not accept her way of life or the fact she was un-married with a child by a drug dealer. Keisha's parents owned a church in Texas so they were very strict about many things, Keisha wasn't prepared to hear the preaching from her parents so she just stayed away, she didn't call, write she just left well enough alone. Denise wasn't too happy that her son still hadn't made Keisha his wife. She couldn't see what the procrastination was all about, they had been together for a long time, moved out of state together and had a child. Denise wasn't going to press the issue she knew that if Divine hadn't made that decision yet it had to be for a reason, so she just kept her opinion to herself.

Watch your Back Chapter 10

Infinity was working the club scene hard, the money was good and the track was starting to get too crazy on the track. She hadn't spoken to Divine in months, he hadn't been in New York in a while and every time she would call his phone she would get the box. Infinity felt like he was avoiding her and was thinking about going down to Florida and shutting his ass down by telling Keisha everything, but she wasn't going to do that just yet. One night in the club she was selected for a private dance, by a dude who looked very familiar to her, she couldn't remember exactly where she knew him from. After the dance was over, he asked her to come back to his hotel room to chill. Infinity knew what he wanted and made sure he knew it would cost him. Once they got to the room, he started to ask her questions about how she got down. Infinity kept her responses short until he asked her had she ever killed somebody. She didn't understand why he was asking so many questions and why did he want to know if she ever killed someone before. He didn't look like a cop and she knew he wasn't a trick. Infinity sat on the bed trying to remember where she knew him from. The only person she had killed was Quan but that was a while ago and only a few people had known about that night. After a few minutes of complete silence, the dude revealed who he was. "Remember me bitch? Raymond asked as he pulled out a gun and pointed at Infinity's head. "Better yet do you remember my cousin? Infinity stood in the room speechless as she tried to figure out how she was going to get out of the room. What she didn't know was that Raymond had been asking around about her and Exstacy and found up what club she worked in and was waiting for the right moment to get at her. Raymond cocked the gun back, Infinity stood in front of him emotionless. "I guess you gotta handle your business," she said without even blinking. "Oh you a bold bitch ain't you, naw I'm not going to kill you at least not yet but you are going to tell me why the fuck you and that other bitch did what you did? Raymond knew that there was someone else behind his cousin's murder. "That was business" Infinity replied without hesitation, Raymond grabbed her by her neck. "Oh it was business, well who the fuck put you up to that business" Infinity didn't flinch and she wasn't going to give Ace or Divine up. "look I'm not no snitch ass bitch, so if you're going to shoot me than handle your business or get that fucking gun out my face! "Don't tempt me" Raymond hit Infinity with the butt of his gun. "Look that nigga did some grimy shit, he had to get got! that's all I'm going to say" Raymond was tired of Infinity getting smart so he placed the gun in her mouth. "Bitch I will blow your fucking brains out! You can either suck on these bullets or answer my question" Infinity wasn't about to die for no nigga especially one who was trying to play her, so she gave Raymond the info he wanted. Raymond had her call Divine, as always she got his voicemail. So she kept calling, finally he picked up. "Hello" Infinity knew she had to act like herself on divine would suspect something. "What you not fucking with me anymore? "Look, I'm busy what's up? Divine wasn't in the mood and didn't want to be bothered. "I need to see you soon, I'm having a problem with this trick" Divine wasn't buying it. "and you calling me for that, call Ace, shit I thought you could handle yourself? Infinity was trying to keep her cool but Divine was pissing her off.

"D! Stop playing with me, after all the shit I did for you, you going to sit up here and play me like this." Infinity was hurt, she had a gun to her face and divine was on the other end of the phone acting like he really didn't give a fuck about her. "Look I'll be up there in a few days; where you going to be at? "just call me when you get up here" Infinity hung up the phone she wasn't sure if she had did the right thing but her life was on the line so she did what she had to do. Raymond warned her if she tried to get slick he would kill her. A few days later, Divine arrived and called Infinity, she told him to meet her by the warehouses downtown. Raymond got in position to wait in the cut for Divine to pull up. An hour later Divine was pulling up to the warehouses, he didn't see Infinity so he parked and started to walk behind the buildings. There he saw Infinity she tried to give him an eye signal but it was too late; shots just started flying, Infinity took off running down the street. once the smoke cleared Raymond's was laying on the ground shot and Divine was shot in the leg, Divine was lucky that Raymond's aim game was trash, Divine limped over to him lying on the ground and shot him in his head. Infinity was a few blocks away before Divine caught up to her. Divine pulled up to her pissed off he yelled. "Get the fuck in the car! Infinity knew she had a lot of explaining to do. "D, baby I'm so sorry! Bitch you sorry! I'm almost got killed behind your stupid ass" Infinity started crying hoping it would calm divine down. "You don't understand this nigga, had a gun to my head". Divine wasn't trying to hear anything Infinity had to say, he drove to the hood doctor and got patched up. He couldn't believe Infinity did him like that, he knew he wouldn't be able to trust her again. Later on that night, he dropped Infinity off and got the hell out of New York.

Infinity was pissed; Divine cut her off completely he told her not to call him anymore. She wasn't going to let Divine just up and leave like that. A week later, she packed a bag and she headed to Florida, it was time to put Divine on blast. Hours after landing she checked into a hotel, chilled for a few days and then she left a message on Divine's phone that she would be paying him a visit very soon. Divine listened to the message and ignored the threat. He assumed Infinity was bluffing. The next day the doorbell rang and to his surprise, it was Infinity, Divine shook his head in disbelief as he walked to the door. "What the fuck are you doing here? Infinity smiled as she walked in. "I'm here to see you" Divine grabbed her by her arm to keep her from walking through the house. "You're really fucking playing with me right now! "What! You don't want that bitch to know about us" Infinity walked around the house; yelling out Keisha's name but Divine told her that Keisha wasn't there. Infinity told him the only way she would leave was if he had sex with her one last time. Divine knew he would be playing it close because Keisha would be home soon but if having sex with her would make her leave then why not do it and get it over with. Once they were finished, he took Infinity back to her hotel room to make sure she checked out and headed to the airport. Infinity left with a smile; little did he know she had a better plan on her mind. Divine headed back to the house to try to clean up before Keisha got home. He pulled into the driveway and quickly ran in the house; he lit some candles and freshened up everything from the carpet to the curtains trying to cover up Infinity's perfume scent. Keisha walked in, impressed to see that he had candles lit, she assumed he was trying to set the mood. She walked upstairs to take a shower and get ready for dinner. Divine walked into the kitchen to get the kitchen right, he noticed Infinity's G-string lying on the floor; he quickly picked it up and put it outside in the trash. Keisha started making dinner and didn't really pick up on Divine's acting strange. After dinner, he gave Keisha a full body massage. "You must want something," Keisha said as she enjoyed the special attention. "Maybe I do" Divine worked Keisha right in the mood. The next day Divine called Infinity to let her know he would be making a trip soon, no matter how hard he tried he couldn't leave her alone. Infinity wanted more from Divine than some dick and shopping sprees, she knew he wasn't going to leave Keisha to be with her, not by choice anyway. Months had went by and Keisha had some news for Divine she was pregnant. Divine was happy to know and so was Denise, Keisha hoped it would be a girl this time around but it was too early to find out. Divine was planning to make one last trip to NY to set his soldiers up with his connect, before he left the game alone. Financially he was where he wanted to be and he invested some money in a few businesses so he was straight. He promised one of his boys he would hand everything over to him, he was also planning to cut Infinity off because if he wasn't going to be in the game the only purpose she would serve would be some ass and he got that from home. Keisha's being pregnant again made Divine want to change his ways a lot, he stopped taking Infinity's calls he hoped she would get tired and leave him alone. Keisha's belly was getting big, she wasn't working at the shop as much, Divine was spending more time at home and Denise was there to help out as much as she could. Divine finally took his mother's advice and asked Keisha to marry him and she yes. Denise offered to help with the wedding planning.

Divine didn't want to set a date until he was finished handling his business in New York.

****

Infinity was getting real pissed with Divine not taking her calls she had a few surprises of her own planned for him. She wasn't working in the club anymore and was staying away from the track; she found herself a group of moneymakers and started pimping them. The days of taking the girls back to Ace were over Infinity was getting it in. She got a nice little crib uptown and even helped Exstacy get into rehab and promised to look out for her once she got herself together. Divine decided to go to New York. As soon as he got there, he called Infinity; she gave him the address to her apartment. When he got there, the first thing he noticed was Infinity's stomach. "What the fuck is this? He asked as he rubbed her belly. What the fuck do you think it is? Infinity said as she pushed her hand off her stomach. "It's not mines" Divine wasn't about to let Infinity trap him up with a baby. "Why wouldn't it be yours, you was fucking me". Infinity knew Divine didn't believe her, it was written all over his face. "Like I was the only nigga" Infinity always used protection with her tricks so she knew it was his. "Nigga stop playing with me! Divine added up the months in his head and knew it could be possible. He couldn't deal with the thought of Keisha finding out, Infinity looked around the same amount of months as Keisha if not further along. "How many months are you? Divine asked hoping she wouldn't be too far along to get an abortion. "How many months ago did we fuck? Infinity tried to kiss Divine he pushed her away. "You are not having this baby; I thought you was too fly to have a kid." Infinity knew Divine had a point, but she had her own reasons for having this baby, Divine told Infinity he wasn't fucking with her anymore and that she was on her own with her decision. He walked out of the apartment and wasn't planning on returning. Infinity was extremely pissed, she someone to do her a favor for a nice amount of cash. Divine was a few blocks away, when Infinity called his phone crying begging him to come back to the house. she made up a story about a clinic she heard about out of town that would perform abortions for pregnancies that were over six months, Divine told her he was on his way back home and wasn't planning to return but would think about it if she was serious about getting an abortion. Infinity promised that she would and she would get it done next week, Divine agreed to come back; he wanted to make sure she was going to go through with it. When Divine got home, Keisha was on the couch crying, she was in a lot of pain. He knew it was too early for her to be in labor but he took her to the hospital to make sure everything was all right with the baby, the doctor did an ultrasound and ran some tests everything was okay but he put Keisha on bed rest. Divine knew it would be hard for him to go back to New York now with Keisha being sick; a week later Divine made up a story about one of his boy's getting locked up, and how he needed to get up there to bond him out. Keisha didn't want him to go, but he promised her it would be his last trip. Divine headed to the airport, he called Infinity to let her know he was on his way, once he arrived he headed straight to Infinity's apartment. When Divine got there Infinity was acting as if she didn't want to go at first but after he threatened to leave she got Dressed and gave him the directions to where the clinic was supposed to be. When they pulled up to the address, Infinity told Divine to stay in the car while she went to go make sure the place was open. Before Divine could question Infinity, she reached over, kissed him on his face, and got out of the car. Divine didn't even notice the man walking up behind the car. (BANG,BANG,BANG) the shots ripped through Divine's chest and his temple. Divine was gone and there was no coming back. After everything he been through with the game, losing his crew, being locked up and beating the system he had fell victim to the one thing he never thought he would fall victim to. Infinity walked over to the car and looked at Divine's lifeless body and said the last words she would ever say to him "power of pussy mother fucker" she drove off with the man she paid to kill Divine and didn't look back. Infinity felt it had to be done since Divine made it clear he wasn't going to be with her, he sure as hell wasn't going to be with Keisha or anybody else. Later on, that night Denise kept trying tried to get Divine on the phone but kept getting his voicemail, she wanted him to know Keisha was in labor. After hours of getting the machine Denise started to get worried, "where is he" she thought to herself. Keisha was angry that Divine was nowhere to be found. she gave birth two months earlier than expected to a 6 lb. 6 oz. baby boy, another son, since Divine wasn't around to name his son Keisha decided to name him Justice, A name that had a special meaning to her and him. A week had passed and Keisha still had not heard from Divine. She and the baby were home and she was starting to wonder if Divine was ok. Keisha walked in the kitchen to make a bottle and the phone rung, to her surprise it was Ace; he had some bad news. Keisha knew something was wrong by the tone of Ace's voice. "Hello Keisha, are you sitting down? Ace's voice had started to crack. "Why Ace what's going on? "It's about D, one of his boys just called me and told me D got shot up" Keisha started to panic. "Shot up oh my god is he alright" Ace could barely respond without breaking down. "No Keisha, D is dead". Keisha dropped the phone and started screaming. Denise was upstairs with the kids, she ran downstairs when she heard Keisha scream. "What's the matter Keisha, why are you crying? "He's gone Denise, Divine is dead" for a minute it didn't register to Denise what Keisha had just said. "What! Wait a minute, not my son, not my child." Denise started crying, she couldn't believe her only child was gone, Divine Jr. woke up from all of the noise and came downstairs, neither one of them could bring themselves to tell him his father was dead.

****

Everyone in the hood was shocked to hear about Divine's death. Keisha arranged for Divine to be buried in New York. A lot of people came to his funeral to pay their respects including Jeremiah who couldn't bring himself to believe that Divine was dead. Infinity heard about the funeral but didn't go, she didn't have any regrets about what she had done. After the burial; Keisha, Denise and the kids went back home. A week had passed and the police didn't have any leads, Keisha wasn't taking that to well she knew someone knew something but wasn't talking. Keisha spent most of her nights crying herself to sleep, trying to picture life without Divine, every day was a challenge, she would have her good days and her bad ones but she tried to stay strong for her boys. Denise dealt with her son's death differently she spent more time with her grandchildren, they reminded her so much of their father, having them around and seeing them grow kept a smile on her face.

169

It had been two month's since Divine's death; Infinity was in the hospital giving birth, she named her baby girl Goddess. Infinity stared at her daughter knowing that she was the reason she would never know her father. A few weeks later Infinity took Goddess to the portrait studio and she decided to mail a picture to Keisha, on the back of the picture, she wrote, "take a good look" Goddess resembled Divine a lot. When Keisha got the picture in the mail, she didn't know what to think, the one thing that caught her attention was that the baby resembled her children. Keisha wondered who mailed her the picture since the envelope didn't have a return address. Keisha needed answers and she knew if anyone had them it would be Ace, she decided to make a special trip to New York. Once she arrived, she headed straight to Ace's house. Ace knew by the look on her face it wasn't a friendly visit. "Hey Keisha" Keisha looked at Ace as if she wanted to slap him. "Don't hey Keisha me, who the fuck is this? Keisha asked as she pulled the picture from her bag.

"You asking me like I know" Ace was being honest, he didn't know who the child was but he could see the child looked like Divine. "You and Divine were close, and I know you would know if he was fucking anybody so tell me! He's dead now and it's nothing he can say so I'm asking you to be honest with me." Ace sat down and stared at the picture. "Well every time D came up here, it was for business, the only one that I knew of him fucking around with was" Ace paused. Keisha was starting to get upset as she waited to hear whom Ace was going to say. "Who was it Ace? Ace walked over to the bar to pour himself a drink. "You already know who Keisha, Divine was messing with Infinity" Keisha looked at Ace and thought he had his information wrong.

"You mean before we went to Florida right? Ace didn't answer, he could tell she didn't know about Infinity and Divine. "wait a minute I know he didn't fuck her after we moved" Keisha took a pause to see if there were any signs that she may have missed but he always acted like his normal self, yeah he spent a lot of time gone but was he really fucking Infinity. "Where is she? I'll ask her myself" Keisha grabbed her bag and walked towards the door; Ace yelled out. "She stays uptown somewhere but she doesn't have a baby" Keisha looked back at him and said; "we'll know in a minute won't we" Keisha stormed out the door and decided to drive uptown to see if she could find Infinity, after asking around she was lucky enough to get an address she headed over there. Infinity was in her apartment putting her daughter down for a nap when she heard a bang on the door. She walked to the door yelling at the person on the other side to stop banging on the door. When she opened it up, she was shocked to see Keisha. "What the fuck are you doing here? Keisha stood in the doorway looking Infinity up and down. "Bitch I'm here to ask you one thing? Infinity laughed aloud. "And what would that be? "You fucked Divine after we moved" Infinity smiled. "Yes I did on plenty occasion's too and he loved every minute in this pussy" Keisha opened up her bag, "oh really so who baby is this in this? Infinity snatched the picture and grinned. "Who does she look like? Keisha grabbed Infinity by her hair and started fighting with her in the apartment. Keisha couldn't believe Divine did her like that, of all bitches to cheat on her with he fucked Infinity and got her pregnant after he promised her he would leave her alone. Keisha punched and kicked Infinity with everything in her body the only thing that stopped her was the sound of a baby crying.

171

Keisha grabbed her bag and rushed out of the apartment. Everything hit her at once. How could he do this to her, she was devoted to him, they were supposed to get married. All the love she had in her heart was replaced with anger. After Keisha left the apartment, Infinity washed her face threw on some clothes and took her baby to one of her girl's house. She knew Keisha would be heading back to Florida and she wanted to be right behind her. Keisha drove to the cemetery; it was something she needed to do before she left. Keisha stood over Divine's headstone and called him everything but the son of god before she walked away she spit on his grave and swore to never come back. After leaving the cemetery Keisha headed to the airport to go back home. She knew Denise would want to know what happened but she wasn't going to tell her. Keisha made it home and went straight to bed she didn't bother to wake Denise up. The next day she called her salon, to let her stylist's know she wouldn't be coming in. she asked Denise if she could take the boys to her house because she wanted some alone time. Keisha looked around the house and everything reminded her of Divine, she pulled down every picture of him even the big one with her and Divine Jr. she screamed, she cried she cut up some of his clothing. A few hours later, the doorbell ranged; Keisha walked to the door and couldn't believe it was Infinity. "How did she know where they lived at" Keisha wondered as she walked into the kitchen and got a knife, she hid it behind her back and opened the door. "How the hell do you know where I live? Keisha asked as she stood in the doorway. Infinity smiled as she pushed the door all the way open. "Oh because I have been here a few times before" Keisha couldn't believe what she was hearing. "Bitch you was in my house?

172

"Yes I was all up in your shit! Keisha pulled the knife from behind her back and tried to stab Infinity, but Infinity took the knife and started to stab her. Keisha couldn't do anything but scream out as Infinity stabbed her up. Infinity kicked her all in her face, her head. After she was finished, she leaned down next to Keisha and whispered. "Now you can join you're your trifling ass baby father bet you didn't know I'm the reason that nigga is dead. Infinity got up from the floor, kicked Keisha one last time, and ran out of the house. Keisha laid there on the floor for a few minutes to make sure Infinity wasn't coming back in. when she realized she was alone she crawled to the phone and dialed 911, the dispatcher couldn't make out what she was saying but it was enough to send a medical unit along with the police to the house. Keisha was losing a lot of blood as she laid there waiting for the ambulance to arrive. the medical team rushed in and put her on the stretcher, once at the hospital and after hours of surgery Keisha was still alive. Infinity was well on her way back to New York, she assumed she left Keisha dead on the kitchen floor. Denise drove to the house to check on Keisha, as she pulled up a neighbor ran over to her and told her Keisha had been taken to the hospital. Denise first thought was that Keisha tried to kill herself, when she arrived the doctors informed her Keisha was brought in with multiple stab wounds. A few days later Keisha was up and able to talk, she told Denise that she got into an altercation with a girl from the shop. Keisha wasn't about to tell Denise what really happened and that her son cheated on her and had another child. Keisha's healing process took a few months; she had gone back to work and appeared to be taking things well. In the back of her mind Infinity's words still burned her, along with

What Divine had done. Infinity was up in New York doing her thing and profiting off her moneymakers, never once did she think that Keisha was still alive or regret what she did. Infinity decided to send goddess to live with her aunt in the Bronx; she wasn't feeling the motherly thing anymore. Infinity never wanted kids and the only reason she had Goddess was to get back at Divine but then it all back fired on her, Divine was dead and she was stuck with a reminder of him; the man she once fucked with hard and had murdered. Ace had moved to Long Island and settled down with a female half his age. He wanted a fresh start; he blamed himself, for Divine getting caught up with Infinity. Ace hadn't seen Infinity in a long time, he wondered if she had anything to do with Divine being shot, but the word he got was that it was a deal gone bad. He never knew or thought Infinity played a major part in Divine's murder.

****

Exstacy was clean and out of rehab, now she was able to focus on her life and everything she had done. She decided to get herself together without Infinity's help. She called her aunt in Virginia and asked could she send her a ticket for her to get down there. When she arrived at the port of Authority she was Stacy a girl who had a hard knock life and got caught up, She quickly realized she still had a chance to do something good with her life and that's what she was going to do.

Seek and you shall find chapter 11

It had been 3 years since Divine's death; Divine Jr. was in the third grade and Justice was in preschool. The decorations in the house were still the same. Keisha was starting to get over her pain, her loss and her anger with Divine and ready to put it all behind her. She decided it was time to redecorate the house, remove Divine's things out of the house, and donate them to a shelter. Divine's closet was packed with clothing and shoes that he barely wore. As she pulled all his clothes off the hangers and removed all of his shoes, she noticed the paint on one section of the wall in the closet was a different color than the rest of the wall. Keisha didn't know why, but her gut feeling was telling her something wasn't right. She got a hammer and a box cutter and began knocking a hole in the wall. She could not believe what she discovered; Divine had packed large amounts of money inside of the wall along with two folders. The first folder had a list of names, places and transactions. The next folder had nude pictures of Infinity along with pictures of her and Divine. Keisha sat on the floor as the tears started rolling down her face. She pulled all of the money out of the wall and began counting. After about 6 hours, she had a total 1 million dollars sitting in front of her. Keisha couldn't believe it all this time, that much money was feet away from her bed. Keisha picked up the folder that contained the names, at the very top of the folder the letters G.M.C were written on the top, she put two and two together and figured these had to be the names of the dudes that worked for Divine. the next page was broken down into codes; which she tried to crack but couldn't really understand, maybe if she would have listened a little more closer to Divine's phone conversations she would have known they were drug code. She put the list to the side and tucked the money under the bed, and placed boxes in front of the wall to cover up the hole. Keisha packed the rest of divine's things, when she opened his drawer she found the key to the safe he had in the basement. she quickly ran down stairs to see what he had hid in there; all she found was old pictures of him and Jb and Quan in younger days and 500 dollars, along with an envelope with her name on it. She opened and it was from Divine.

Dear Keisha,

I know we have had our share of problems, but I need you to know you and my son mean the world to me. No matter what you may think, everything I did I did for us, I made many mistakes in my life but I never meant to hurt you. No matter what happens, take care of my son and yourself. Don't let anyone put any crazy shit in your head about me or my feelings for you. Love always Divine"

Keisha threw the letter down, "when the hell did he write this?" she thought to herself because the letter wasn't dated. She wasn't sure why was he wrote a bunch of lies to her acting like he loved her when he knew all along he was fucking Infinity, Keisha couldn't believe it and all the pain was building up all over again, it was time to pick the boys up. so she hurried up out the door, at times it was hard for her to even look at her boys because they reminded her so much of their father, Divine Jr. had Divine's charm, his walk and his smile. Justice had his father's personality. Every little thing about Divine that once made her smile now made her cry. She constantly wondered how old Infinity's daughter was and how she looked. She knew eventually Divine Jr. and Justice would be at the age to travel and she hoped they would never bump into their half-sister, Keisha would never forget what Infinity had done to her and if she had her way she would deal with her but she wanted to wait til the time was right. Keisha decided to contact one of Divine's boys to question him about what she had found in the folder. He told her their conversation couldn't be over the phone. A week later Keisha decided to fly up to New York to speak with one Divine's soldiers, things had dried up after Divine was gone. Every soldier that was on his team and was getting money fell off because Divine never had the chance to set up everything with his connects. Little did Keisha know she held the key to it all. She met up with Dre, one of the younger dudes that was down for it all when it came to Divine. He explained the codes to her to the best of his ability. he also told her how the connects weren't fucking with anyone because they didn't think anyone could be trusted after what happened to D, Keisha knew who killed Divine and by the way Dre was talking she knew that he didn't know, "do you have a number for a connect? "No but if you have all that info right there, then it should be in there" Keisha looked through each of the pages thoroughly until she came across a page with numbers written down. Dre told her to dial the first one she saw. After a few rings, a man answered the phone, he knew who ever called him was had to be real close to Divine because Divine never gave numbers out. Keisha spoke briefly to the male on the other end of the phone, she was giving an address to meet with him, she wasn't too sure if it was safe to go by herself but he told her to come alone.

177

Once she arrived, a female in a black car told her to get in the car with her, they drove a few miles and then she met the connect his name she never knew but he was very up front. He asked Keisha how did she find his information and Keisha told him about the folder being hidden in the wall after he verified her information, he told her that Divine told him if anything ever happened to him that every and anything should be giving to her. She couldn't believe that "how is that possible? She asked. He was supposed to hand everything over to one of his boys. "Well he never gave me a name none other than yours in our last conversation." Keisha was blown. "So what the hell and I'm supposed to get? The connect got up and walked over to his safe. "Well let's see I owed him some things large quantities, so now it's yours! Now if you want I can buy it from you and that will be the end of it or you can take it handle your business" Keisha shook her head. "My business, you expect me to sell drugs! "I'm just giving you options" Keisha sat there quietly for a few minutes trying to figure out why Divine left everything to her and why would he want her to get in the game. She also wondered about Infinity and why he didn't leave the street shit to her. Keisha decided to take the product and work with it the best way she could. She never wanted to be a hustler that was Divine's thing but now he was gone. She contacted Dre and told him she needed him to meet with her and bring a few soldiers. She wasn't sure how they would take the news she had to give, but once they arrived she let them know what went down with the connect and how she was giving the ok to handle things. A few members of Divine's team couldn't believe what was going down and felt some kind of way. Dre quickly reminded them that without her they would still be scrambling. Keisha was now in charge and she was getting that paper and keeping it. Keisha put Dre in charge of pick up and distribution she would just handle the money. Word spread quickly around the hood about Keisha being in New York. Infinity didn't believe what she was hearing because she left her on the floor a second away from death. Infinity asked around and got the word that Keisha was running all of Divine's business. Infinity was pissed, she felt that was her position and Keisha didn't have what it took to run anything. Divine trusted Keisha with more than his heart. Keisha finally got her chance to handle Infinity. she saw her coming out of the club and she ran up on her. Infinity didn't blink or jump as she saw Keisha running up behind her. "What bitch you coming back for more? You ain't get enough from the last time? Keisha walked up to Infinity and pulled out a gun, she didn't even think twice.(BANG,BANG,BANG) Infinity's body fell to the ground. Keisha walked back to her car, and drove off, without a worry in the world. No one at the club saw what had happened but everyone heard the shots. Keisha headed to the airport and carried as if nothing happened. Keisha didn't want to be a hustler, she had seen for herself what hustling could do to a family, a relationship, a friendship so she passed everything over to Dre, connect information and all. Dre was more than happy to take over and out of Divine's soldier's he was more reliable and trustworthy. She knew that if Divine had his say he most likely would have picked Dre as well. Once Keisha got back home, she decided to pack everything up and move. Even though she loved her house and all the good times her and Divine shared, it also had bad memories. The thought that Divine slept with Infinity all up in there just made Keisha sick to her stomach,

179

Divine's Justice

she sold the house and signed her shop over to Denise. With all the money she had, she was able to make a fresh start and put everything behind her. She decided to drive down to Texas and see her parents to heal all wounds, and let her boys meet their grandparents for the first time. Keisha vowed never to look back and to keep her boys away from the game at all cost. She was through with the lifestyle and all the drama that came along with it.

THE GAME WILL GO ON

Dre picked up where Divine left off as far as the game was concerned. He was doing his thing; he had the hood on lock and was on top of the world. He made sure to be cautious of everything and everyone because he had seen a lot of hustlers rise and a lot of hustlers fall and he was determined to ride it out on top of the world until the end. Even though Divine was gone the game wasn't over. Hustling played a major part in every hood. Who ever thought that three little niggas from the hood who started out getting money with candy bars would have turned into kingpins, the G.M.C. crew had their time and they shined well but every cookie crumbles. in every city and every hood, the hustle lives on and if you're going to get down with it you need to stay focus and never trust anyone but yourself because one mistake can cost you your life.

****

This book is Dedicated to all the falling soldiers who fell victim to the game city to city, hood to hood, worldwide and all the women who loved them , R.I.P Pee- Wee, Doobie, Manny, Doe Boy, Jb, 36th street family, free Preme a.k.a Jahmel one love   S. W

About The Author

Brooklyn Native, Shameeka; The Bunny behind the Hustle is no stranger to the game. She has lived it; she has loved it, even suffered from it. After losing friends and family members to the streets and the system, she felt the only way to deal with her pain was to write, not only to heal but also to get her stories out. Faced with the fears of rejection from the industry, she decided to get her hustle on and put the work in for herself. Shameeka has always been poetically talented. She started working on Divine's Justice in 2005 after she and her kids were in a tragic car accident that left one of her children disabled. Going through that tough time alone, she felt all she could do instead of crying was to write and that is when the birth of Divine's Justice began.

****

She resides, in Hampton, Virginia, with her children and fiancé. In her spare time, she is working on her second book, Along with many other projects.

ORDER INFO

To purchase a copy of this book send your payment of 13.95 plus 5.00 for shipping and handling to:

Shameeka Williams

P.O. Box 3731

Hampton, Virginia 23663

(Money order or checks only)

You may also purchase a copy directly from my website using pay pal or on amazon.com the link is listed on the website;

http://divinesjustice.weebly.com

For orders shipped to prisons but not limited to federal, state or county. The price of the book is 12.00 shipping and handling will be free.